She tried the door, and it opened; the catch wasn't down. The light inside shone very brightly as she pushed the door open wider. Something caught at her nerves, like a hand clutching at her. She was afraid of what she might find, frightened to go in. Her breath came in short, sharp gasps.

'Don't be a coward!' she exclaimed aloud, and thrust the door back and strode in.

May Sharp lay on the bed, with her throat cut. The pillows and sheets were soaked in the hideous red of blood.

Also by the same author,
and available in Coronet Books:

**The Baron Series**

# The Baron Goes Fast

John Creasey
**as Anthony Morton**

CORONET BOOKS
Hodder Paperbacks Ltd., London

Copyright 1954 by John Creasey
First published 1954
by Hodder and Stoughton Ltd
Coronet edition 1960
Third impression 1973

---

Printed in Great Britain
for Coronet Books, Hodder Paperbacks Ltd.,
St Paul's House, Warwick Lane, London, EC4P 4AH.
by Richard Clay (The Chaucer Press), Ltd.,
Bungay, Suffolk

ISBN 0 340 02486 0

# CONTENTS

# 1

# THE SHADOWS

THE woman came out of the tall, dark building in the Strand, and walked towards Fleet Street. She was tall and good to look at. The skirt of her grey suit rode up the back of her legs and drew attention to them; they were slim, a nice shape, and with neat ankles. She had the kind of figure that the suit couldn't hide, and probably her tailor hadn't tried very hard. She also wore a white blouse, with frilly cuffs and sleeves, and a small white hat with a veil which served only one purpose: decoration.

She walked well if impatiently; as if the narrow skirt were proving a nuisance.

She was nice-looking, although not remarkable, and had beautiful, impressive, almost startlingly blue eyes. Her make-up was just right.

When she reached the narrow stretch of road by the Law Courts, with their pale grey towers and lordly aloofness, she must have passed at least a thousand people; at least a dozen of the men had looked at her intently, and most of them had thought: "American, of course, you can tell 'em a mile off." Then, according to their nature and their temperament, they had dreamed fleeting dreams about her.

She stopped, to cross the road, and glanced to the left, the direction from which she had come. Her lips closed tightly, before she looked away.

A man, short, stout, carelessly dressed in a sports jacket and flannels which hadn't been pressed for weeks, smiled at her back. He was bare-headed, and his pate had a wispy covering of browny hair, more like down than the hair of a man's head. In some lights, he probably looked bald. His face was round and fleshy, his mouth full but small. At a casual glance, people often thought him a pleasing type; genial, benevolent, kindly. No one ever made a greater mistake.

The woman crossed the road, and the man followed her.

There was a change in her movements, now, a jerkiness; she had become self-conscious and keenly aware of the fact that she was being followed. Nearing Chancery Lane, she saw a policeman, hot in his navy serge and tall helmet. She avoided his eye. Being a man, he looked her up and down, doubtless thinking: "That's a nice bit of stuff," or something to that effect.

The woman turned into Chancery Lane. By a shop with its window crammed with legal tomes bound in dark leather and unexpectedly ticketed *Sale Price*, she glanced round. The short, stout man smiled at her, and would have looked cherubic but for a glint in his eyes, then went past the end of Chancery Lane along Fleet Street. The woman raised her tightly clenched hands as high as her high breasts; and for a moment, closed those fine eyes.

Then she walked on, quickly, agitatedly, as if feeling that she was being followed by the man's shadow. In an odd way, her progress had become a flight. She was interested only in what lay behind her, not what lay ahead. But it was something in front which jolted her next — a man, tall, thin, sneering, with a long pointed nose, who stepped into her path from the doorway of an office building.

She had to stop, backed, looked at him — and saw the sneer. It was almost a grin, but it did not touch the man's eyes.

8

"Why don't you turn it in?" he asked.

She pushed past him — actually pushed him out of her way. Perhaps it was the sight of others in the narrow street which stopped him from reprisals. He turned and watched her, and his eyes were narrowed and the look in them was not good.

She reached High Holborn, swarming with traffic and people, the traffic dominated by the great red buses which seemed to move so slowly, in contrast to the box-like taxis darting about like agitated robot ants. She glanced round, from the corner. The man was standing in the doorway, grinning; she could see his long, narrow teeth. She turned abruptly, and nearly bumped into a youth.

He said:

"Going any place, sister?"

He was by a shop window at the corner, sleek, young, black hair heavy with oil and glistening in the sunlight, but loose and waving. It framed his face, made his wrinkled forehead narrow, and made his small ears look white.

"Why don't you come along with me?" he asked.

He spoke with a nasal whine, aping an American accent and sounding as phony as anyone could. He put out a hand and touched her arm, but the woman snatched herself free and strode on, skirt riding. She didn't get far.

The tall man had hurried past her, and was now just in front, in her way again.

The short, stout man was approaching too; obviously he had come a long way round so as to meet her here. Now she was hemmed in by all three. But no one passing would have thought of 'hemmed in'. In fact a policeman going off duty saw them, and wondered what the handsome woman was doing with three types like that, but had no cause to suspect that they were using pressure; or

9

uttering menaces. Not in High Holborn, in broad daylight!

"Give it up, Helen," the short, stout man said in a smooth, English voice, the voice of an educated man. "You can't get away with it."

"Just turn it in," said the tall man.

"See it our way," chimed in the youth with the oily hair, chewing steadily on gum which he showed whenever he opened his mouth. He had big eyes, like over-ripe black cherries, and a sallow face – the look of South Europe and the voice of an Americanised Cockney. "You won't come to no harm," he mocked her. "How about a little ride, sister?"

She didn't speak but looked up and down, desperately; there was no other word. She was seeking help, but in a hunted way which made it clear that she expected none. She was no longer in flight, but at bay.

The short, stout man said: "Robbie will only get hurt."

"Real bad," said the youth.

"See it our way," urged the tall man, "he'll love you even more for it! Come on, now."

The woman's wonderful eyes were so bright that it was as if she had a fever. Her lips looked dry, even when she moistened them. Her hands were clenched inside her white gloves, and raised – but that was from tension, not because she was ready to strike any of them.

"I don't know a thing," she said hoarsely, "not a thing."

"Now listen," began the youth.

"Nor does Robbie," she interrupted him, and suddenly seemed breathless. "You've got the wrong man, you – "

The tall man took her wrist. To passers-by it was just a casual gesture. The youth and the short stout man were smiling, as if this were a friendly little party and all four were talking about pleasant things; but the bony fingers were tight, and they hurt.

"Forget it," he said nastily. "You've got them, we want them. Listen — we'll tear Robbie apart if you haven't come across by tonight. You be at Piccadilly Circus, see, nine o'clock. By Swan & E's. *And* you'd better have them."

"I haven't got them!" The woman's voice rose, and an elderly man passing glanced at her in surprise, but walked on. "I don't know where they are," she insisted desperately, "and Robbie — "

"It's a pity about Robbie," the short, stout man said smoothly. "Such a nice kid. Good-looking, too. Wouldn't he look different without a nose?"

He smiled.

"No!" the woman gasped.

They all grinned at her, just an innocent little group standing at a corner and talking. As the woman had her back to the passing crowd, few noticed that she was alarmingly pale.

"You wouldn't — " she choked.

"There isn't a thing we wouldn't do, Helen," the short man assured her. "You know it, and there isn't a thing you can do about it. Because we can get Robbie ready for the high jump, and you wouldn't like that, would you? Why don't you give up? You're a good, brave girl. We know about that now. Not many women would have put up a brave fight like yours. That's fine, that's okay. We don't want to hurt you, we don't want to hurt Robbie — but we want the ice. Understand?"

"I don't know where it is," she said, tensely. She knew that 'ice' meant diamonds. "Why don't you believe me?" She was pathetic.

"We're like that," sneered the black-haired youth, "we can tell when anyone's lying, it's second nature to us." His dark eyes looked her up and down insolently. "Just bring that ice along to us tonight."

"Tonight," echoed the thin man.

"Nine o'clock," said the short, stout man abruptly.

They turned away from her, two moving towards Oxford Street, one towards the city. For a few seconds, she stood alone, and quite still. More men took notice of her, now, although she stared in the shop window, seeing nothing but her own reflection.

She let her arms fall by her side, and moved back towards Chancery Lane. She looked everywhere about her, but did not see any of the men. Her breath came in short, sharp gasps; panting breath. Now she was in flight again, but she did not go far. She reached a doorway, the one in which the tall man had been standing, and the building to which she had been going. The long, narrow hall was dark and empty; the stairs were badly lighted. There was a lift opposite the foot of the stairs, the cage somewhere up above, the iron trellis door dusty and dirty. Nearby was a panel with the names and addresses of the tenants on it. There were accountants, architects, solicitors, turf accountants, exporters, and *The Ling Enquiry Agency — Confidential Inquiries Made. Second Floor.*

She pressed the lift bell; nothing happened.

She could walk up two flights.

Now she hurried, and the skirt caught against the back of her legs, and showed the lace hem of her slip. The first landing was lit by subdued daylight coming through a window at the far end of a passage; and through the frosted glass panels of the doors with black lettering on them. She hurried towards the next flight of stairs, went up them, and was already breathing hard, partly from exertion, partly because of the driving fears.

She reached the second-floor landing. Two doors

facing her had top panels of frosted glass and black
lettering:

> The Ling Inquiry Agency
> P. Stocker.
> Confidential Inquiries
> Represented in: New York, Paris, Rome, Buenos Aires.

The landing was dark and shadowy, and no one was
about. The lift was on this floor, the door standing open
so that it could not move. The bell was ringing downstairs; and in one of the offices another bell was ringing,
while from the first door came the sound of voices, of
men, murmuring.

A smaller sign on this door read: *Inquiries*.

The bells kept ringing.

Someone started to walk up the stairs, and the
American woman named Helen was jolted into movement. The moments of indecision were gone. She strode
towards the door marked *Inquiries*, and went in.

Two men were in the room, one on either side of a
dark wooden counter. It was a tiny room, partitioned
off from the main office. The man on the far side of
the counter turned to look at her, and immediately
showed interest; all men would, when seeing her for
the first time. Those eyes made sure of it.

The second man, with his back to her, also turned;
and grinned.

It was the tall man.

The woman felt the little colour that she had left
draining from her cheeks. It was as if all the blood in
her veins was being emptied out, taking her courage
and her hope with it.

"Hallo, sister," said the tall man, jeeringly, "why
don't you wait outside, like a good girl?"

"I –"

"I'm making all the arrangements," he said, and
grinned at her again – and also commanded.

She turned and went out, on to the gloomy landing. One bell had stopped, but the other was still ringing. She was trembling; shivering. There was silence on the stairs until she moved forward, and then footsteps came, slowly; of a man, coming up.

They met half-way.

It was the oily-haired youth.

"Had a nice little chat with Pip Stocker?" he asked. "Or did Dan get in first?"

She rushed past him. He stood and grinned after her, but there was little mirth in his expression. He didn't hurry, though. She reached the street again, and she felt worse, much worse, than she had all day; and she had been frightened most of the day.

She reached the street.

The short, stout man with the air of false benevolence was standing just outside, smoking a cigarette, hands in his pockets. He shot her a sly, sideways glance, and said:

"Give it up, Helen. Be sensible. Just turn the stuff over, and you'll get your Robbie back and everything will be fine. No trouble at all. We aren't spiteful, we won't hold anything against you – *or* Robbie. Bring the ice to us tonight, at nine o'clock."

"*I don't know where it is!*"

He just grinned at her, but his eyes threatened, and they were the kind of eyes one would expect a snake to have.

She caught her breath and turned away and hurried back towards the busy Strand, the grey, indifferent Law Courts and the policeman on duty.

The man followed her, watching the way her skirt rode up her shapely legs as she hurried in a flight from the inescapable.

14

# 2

# WORD FROM A STRANGER

HELEN CHADWICK told herself that she was crazy to keep looking round, that it did no good, and only showed the men that she was terrified. As if they didn't know already! She couldn't do a thing to help herself, and what seemed worse just then, not a thing to help Robbie. It was like a nightmare, in spite of the warm sun and the hurrying people so preoccupied with their own affairs. It *was* a nightmare; the kind of thing one only knew about vicariously, from newspapers and 'True Crime' stories and that unreal world. In the newspapers and magazines it was sheer melodrama, but today she felt the cold hands of fear; of dread.

The hard thing to believe was that Robbie was bad.

She reached Woolworth's in the Strand, and joined the queue for the bus; only half-a-dozen people were waiting. The crowd on the pavement got thicker, and men jostled her. Accidentally? Had those three men allies whom she didn't know?

Traffic was thicker. Those huge red buses lorded it over private cars, the goods vehicles and the cabs with their dignified impudence. The buses fascinated her when she had first reached London, but now she took them for granted, like everything else. She waited for a Number 15, got on and half ran up the narrow stairs while the bus was moving. She stared down, but no one followed her; not one of the three men who had persecuted her for days appeared to have followed.

But one of them had, she was sure; he would be in a taxi, nearby, on another bus or in a private car. They had not let her alone at all since the campaign had begun.

She looked down from the top of the bus, seeing no familiar, sinister face.

It was always better when none of them was in sight; she felt that she could breathe; it was as if some kind of physical pressure had been eased. She opened her black calf bag, took out cigarettes, and lit one; it was the last in the pack of Pall Mall, and she crumpled the shiny red paper up and let it drop to the floor.

She watched the passing pageant of London; the pigeons and the sightseers in Trafalgar Square, the bronze lions; the tall column which seemed to stretch into the sky, too tall for her to see the figure at the top from here. The fountains were playing. Everyone in the Square seemed to have plenty of time, while everyone in the surrounding streets seemed to be in a hurry. She caught a glimpse of the Mall, through Admiralty Arch.

Robbie had shown her round London, told her everything, been as efficient as a guide in a Cook's Tour — but nervous, as if on the point of confession, before he had disappeared.

The bus went slowly, stopped time and time again; it seemed incapable of reaching her journey's end. But she reached it — Oxford Street, near the Circus. She hurried down the stairs, long legs scurrying. Men stared at her, eyes brightening. She looked about her and saw no one whom she knew; the relief was almost painful, but experience had told her that she could not be certain yet.

She crossed the road with a throng of people, then took a side street, towards the private hotel where she was staying. No one followed her, no one turned into the street. Her room overlooked this street, and she went straight up to the window and peered out.

A man walked briskly from the corner, as if knowing exactly what he wanted, and disappeared into the hotel entrance, but that was nothing to do with her.

She dropped into a chair by the window, and closed her eyes.

It wasn't much of a room; about fifteen feet square. There was a double bed with a single pillow, a wardrobe that had a piece of shiny wood falling out at one side, a wash-basin, a chest of drawers with a mirror perched on top; but it was both cheap and central, and she hadn't much money – now.

A clock struck and she opened her eyes, listened and counted.

". . . four . . . five."

The three men, so different to look at, so identical in manner and in evil purpose, seemed to be crowding round her again. She had orders to go and see them at nine o'clock tonight; in four hours' time. She was to take the 'ice' – that was, the diamonds they believed that Robbie had given to her. They had even taught her a new vernacular. It was a simple story, but in some ways so ugly. She did not want to believe it, but there was little doubt that Robbie had stolen the 'ice', and they had blackmailed him, or tried to; and afterwards kidnapped –

*Kidnapped.*

The word took on fresh meaning. It meant an aching feeling of dismay; of despair. It was like someone's death, in a way; an acute awareness of someone's absence; of a familiar face missing. It was fear. It was emptiness.

The telephone bell rang.

The room had few things to commend it, but the telephone was one of the few. It was within her reach, on a small table by the side of the bed. She stared at it. A little colour had come back to her cheeks, but the ringing took it away again. She moistened her lips. They would not let her alone, and she should have known it. They had allowed her to come here without being followed, judged the moment when she would be

17

back, and were starting the persecution again. Sly, ugly, menacing words would be spoken into the telephone, words she could not answer, threats about which she could do nothing because of what the men could do to Robbie. Or said they could do.

The bell rang again.

She shivered, and stretched out her hand slowly, then touched the black instrument. It still rang, and the vibration made her arm quiver. She picked it up.

"Hal – lo?"

"Is that Miss Helen Chadwick," asked a man briskly. She did not recognise the voice, but was sure that it was not one of her three tormentors. That was no cause for relief. They might use others; they knew every trick it was possible to play.

"Yes," she said.

"My name is Stocker, Miss Chadwick. I wonder if you can spare me a few minutes." He was very brisk and very English, with a 'no time for nonsense' manner.

"I don't think we're acquainted, Mr Stocker," Helen said with an effort.

"We are in a way," said the man in that matter-of-fact voice, "and I think I might be of some service to you. I needn't keep you long and you will be under no obligation."

"No, Mr Stocker, I really don't – "

*Stocker.*

In her mind's eye she saw a frosted glass doorway, and some stencilled black wording:

*The Ling Inquiry Agency*
*P. Stocker.*
*Confidential Inquiries*
*Represented in: New York, Paris, Rome, Buenos Aires.*

She also saw the man leaning against the counter in

the partitioned office, half hidden by the tall beast who had turned round and made her leave.

"Stocker," she echoed, "from the Ling Inquiry — "

"That's right, Miss Chadwick."

"How — "

"Miss Chadwick," said the man, not only briskly but earnestly, "I really think that I may be of some service to you and that it would be to your advantage to spare me a few minutes. You can always throw me out!"

She could imagine that he smiled, although he was talking into the telephone. The English often made that kind of remark and smiled as if it were a subtle joke. She had to make up her mind, and although she was still prepared to believe that this was a trick, she also dared to hope.

"All right," she said abruptly. "Where are you?"

"I'm downstairs in the lobby of your hotel," said Stocker. "May I come up and see you?"

"I guess you can," she said. "I'll be waiting."

She put the receiver down on his thanks, and then looked out of the window. No one was in sight, she did not think that any of the three men was here. This Stocker might be genuine; but the tall man had been talking to him, and there was no way of being certain that he was not working for them.

She opened her bag, powdered her cheeks, touched up her nice lips. Her eyes were very bright — she knew that it was partly from nerves. She was used to their brilliance, and could be critical of it. She turned away, brushing powder off her coat. She hadn't moved far before there was a sharp tap at the door.

It was self-locking; she unfastened it, and as she did so told herself that no one had yet troubled her in here, the room had been the one sanctuary. Had she thrown this away? The thump of her heart beats almost hurt.

It wasn't the man who had seen her at the Agency.

This one was smartly dressed, with the curiously well-scrubbed look of some English. He had fair hair, a fresh complexion, clear blue eyes, emphatic features. A youthful thirty-five who might be forty. He was of medium height, lean and hardy-looking: perhaps healthy was the right word. His movements, his manner and his voice had that common feature of briskness.

"Good evening, Miss Chadwick, very good of you to see me." He closed the door, and smiled at her. "*Very* good. I wouldn't have worried you without reason, I assure you."

"I don't understand you," she said.

"I'll soon explain — but won't you sit down? Cigarette?" He offered her cigarettes from a silver case produced from his pocket with an almost military precision. "Can't offer you American cigarettes, I'm afraid." He looked into her eyes, then quickly away; but they affected some men like that.

"I like yours," she said, half-truthfully.

"Can't say I like *yours*," he said lightly, "but I bet I'd soon learn to!"

He lit the cigarettes; then she sat down and he moved to the window.

It was a swift movement, and his glance into the street was very quick — but she had an impression that he wouldn't miss much. Then he turned to face her, so that his back was to the window.

"You are related to Robert Mitch Chadwick, of Glenton, New Jersey, aren't you?"

She had been feeling better, partly because it was almost impossible to associate this man with the other three; they were so obviously different. But on his words, she turned cold. It was a physical change; she felt the coldness creep through her body.

She couldn't answer, her throat was so dry.

"Sister?" asked Stocker abruptly.

She didn't answer.

Stocker drew at his cigarette, then took it from his lips and studied the glowing tip, as if he wanted to save her from the embarrassment of being stared at. He didn't smile, yet managed to give the impression that there was nothing really serious about his business or about his inquiry.

"Let's just say that you're related," he suggested after a pause. "And he's missing, isn't he?"

She said: "I – I don't know how – " and stopped.

"It's a long story," said Stocker, "but perhaps I ought to tell you about it first. I'm on your side, you know!" His smile was boyish, but she was sure that he meant what he said at the time. "As a matter of fact I've been looking for Robert Mitch Chadwick for over a week, and I know you have, too."

Helen started again: "How – " and stopped, because any question seemed superfluous.

"Let's see if I can summarise it for you," said Stocker, with a look suggesting that at all costs he wanted to be fair to her. "I was looking for Chadwick, because I was looking for some jewels he might know something about. I represented the insurance company. I discovered that someone else was making inquiries – including the man who was in my office this afternoon. So I had one of my operatives watch them. After all, they might have had more luck than I, mightn't they? I learned that they were interested in you, and it wasn't difficult to find out your name. *Are* you Chadwick's sister?"

"Yes," Helen said.

"There's a likeness," Stocker told her, examining her more closely, and giving no indication of approval or otherwise.

"Have you *seen* him?" she exclaimed.

"Twice, for a few minutes each time. First when I went to see his employer," Stocker said. "These other people think that your brother stole the Wannaker diamonds, don't they?"

"I don't believe he did!" Helen tried to put conviction into her voice but it wasn't easy. Against all her emotions, she had come to the conclusion that Robbie lied easily; that he would cheat; and if he would cheat her, why shouldn't he cheat and rob others?

"Of course you don't," said Stocker reassuringly. She began to wonder whether this manner wasn't assumed, and whether he wasn't giving her the impression of being a nice, clean-limbed, clean-thinking, unsubtle Englishman because he was anxious that she should not realise how subtle he was. "That isn't quite the question I asked. Do they *think* he stole the diamonds?"

"Yes."

"And they think you know where the diamonds are," Stocker went on calmly. "They'd learned you were coming to see me, and were ready to scare you off. Do you think they've kidnapped your brother?"

"They—yes," she cried, "yes! And I don't know anything about these diamonds." Her fears came out, passionately. "I just don't know. I can't help Robbie. They've threatened—"

She broke off.

"Yes?"

"They've threatened to disfigure him." She fought for control of her voice. "There isn't a thing I can do, I just can't help Robbie, but I must find a way!" When he didn't respond, she added desperately: "There must *be* some way."

"Yes," said Stocker very confidently. "Yes, I think there is. Will you take some advice from me?"

She saw a change in his expression, which puzzled her at first. Then he glanced swiftly towards the door. Her impression, that he was very alert, lively and able, was stronger than ever. He moved swiftly towards the door, without saying a word. He snatched the door open. Helen saw a head of black hair, very wavy and smothered with oil. Next she saw Stocker's arm move, heard a thud followed by a squeal.

The black head vanished as the youth rocked back on his heels.

### 3

### ADVICE

HELEN did not move, but Stocker did, so she was able to see the youth as he banged against the passage wall. His nose was beginning to bleed already. He had no time to move away before Stocker gripped his right wrist. Helen saw the movement and yet was taken by surprise. Stocker moved so swiftly that it was like seeing a film running too fast across the screen; he bent down, his arm moved, he gripped the youth's wrist, drew the youth away from the door and then propelled him into the bedroom.

Then he closed the door, without slamming it.

The youth struck a chair, nearly fell, but kept his balance while swaying. The blood covered his upper lip like raspberry juice, and started to run into his mouth. He looked too frightened to worry about anything else. This smooth-voiced, menacing creature was as scared as she had been. For the first time since she realised what was afoot, she felt — happy. It was a momentary elation and wouldn't last, but it was like a long drink.

"How long were you outside?" Stocker asked, in that same fresh voice.

"I — I only just came."

"Who sent you?"

"I — I wanted to talk to — her." The youth glanced at Helen, and it was hard to believe that these frightened eyes could ever hold such insolence.

"Who are you working for?" Stocker asked, and went on without a pause: "Dizzy?"

"No!" That brought fresh fear. "No, I — I don't know." The hoarse voice became a whine. "I don't *know*."

"Listen to me," said Stocker, "you sneaked in here, you didn't get permission to come upstairs, and you started to pick the lock of this door. That's enough to put you inside, and I'd be happy to tell the beak all about it. Fond of prison life?"

The youth didn't speak.

"Who are you working for?" demanded Stocker, as if quite sure he would get a reply.

"I don't know! — Ben knows."

"Ben?"

The youth licked his lips but didn't explain.

"One of them is called Ben," Helen broke in. "The short fat one."

"I see," said Stocker. He kept talking in a breezy way, as if this were the most ordinary thing to happen; and Helen was now quite sure that it was a pose, but it helped her. The exhilaration hadn't all gone, because the blood was now on the youth's chin, and because she wasn't alone any longer.

Was she?

"So you work for Ben, and you want me to believe that you don't know who's paying him," said Stocker to the youth. He gave the smile of a man who was enjoying himself. "Where's Chadwick?"

"If I told you — "

"I find things out for myself," said Stocker, "and I know that you and your friend Ben and the tall streak snatched Robbie Chadwick. Don't let any harm come to him, or you'll find yourself in a lot of trouble."

24

His smile grew much broader, he had very white, strong-looking teeth. "You make plenty of mistakes, you and your friends," he declared, and took a second off to wink at Helen; it was only a flicker of an eyelid but how it encouraged her! "You don't know who you're up against."

Something that was related to courage crept back into the youth. Perhaps he had recovered from the hurt; perhaps he thought that he wouldn't be attacked again. He dabbed his lips and chin with a handkerchief, and actually squared his shoulders.

"Oh, don't we," he muttered, and it was nearly a sneer. "You won't stop Ben sleeping at nights, Stocker, and the dame knows what will happen to her kid brother if anyone goes to the police. You or the dame. Because we can prove that the kid brother lifted the ice, see."

His gaze shifted from Stocker to Helen and back, as if he suddenly wondered how wise he had been to turn aggressive, and was already half-regretting it.

"The police," echoed Stocker softly, and smiled again. "Why don't you grow up? This isn't a police job — yet." He let that sink in, and obviously the youth didn't like it. "You've much more to worry about than that."

The youth's eyes asked nervously: "What?"

"Listen," said Stocker, briskly, "go back to Ben, tell him you ran into a door unexpectedly, and then ask him if he wants to have trouble with Mannering." He uttered the last word, the name, very softly, and repeated it: "With *Man*nering, I said."

Helen was watching the youth.

He had become a different man in front of her eyes during the past ten minutes. He had been frightened, then bewildered, then aggressive, next, nervous. Now, he stood staring into Stocker's eyes as if he were trying desperately to find out whether the man had told the truth. He closed his eyes, and his lips began to move as if he were muttering some incantation which he hoped would exorcise a devil that now threatened him. What he showed now wasn't the kind of fear that Stocker's violence had put into him; it was a quieter, deeper emotion.

"*Man*nering," he echoed.

"That's right." Stocker took a lot of pleasure in confirming it. "Mannering's on her side, too. Tell Ben."

The youth looked at his bloodstained handkerchief. He seemed to commune with himself for several seconds, and then shot Helen a quick, scared look.

"Okay," he said. "I'll tell Ben."

"And also tell Ben that we want Robbie Chadwick back," said Stocker. "Soon."

"I – I'll tell him. I can't promise – "

"It doesn't matter a damn what you promise," Stocker said. "I wouldn't believe you." He moved with that now familiar speed and precision, and the youth backed away in a flurry of fear. The movement would not have saved him, had Stocker meant to strike; but all Stocker did was to take a wallet from his coat pocket with a speed which was like sleight of hand.

He backed away, holding the yellow leather wallet.

The youth stood, glaring but cowed.

Stocker opened the wallet, and shook two letters on to the bed, with several pound notes, some visiting cards and other oddments. He picked up one of the letters, and read:

"So you're Percy Morino? The name's a bit hybrid, isn't it? And you live in Moon Court. No wonder you don't know what's good for you! Go and tell Ben all about his troubles, Percy."

"I – I want my wallet back!"

"Help yourself," said Stocker generously.

He moved to Helen's side, winked again, and poured

more confidence into her. They watched Morino fumbling for the wallet, the letters and the oddments. He stuffed all these into his pocket, then scurried to the door, looking as if he expected Stocker to stop him at the last minute. But Stocker only rubbed his hands free of imaginary dust, and grinned as the door closed.

"It's all right, we won't lose him," he said to Helen, "one of my operatives is outside. We've been watching you for some time. When I heard that these boys kept you away from the office, I thought it time to tell you about it. Feel better?"

"I really do!" She even felt that she could be confident again. "Thanks to you, Mr Stocker."

"No," Stocker said, emphatically, "little to do with me. I'm just the instrument." His grin was a most attractive one but was it genuine? "Thanks to a certain John Mannering. You don't know him, but you're going to. Of Quinns." He shot that word out, and she sensed that he was watching her as if to find out whether it meant anything to her.

It did not.

"Quinns," repeated Stocker. "That's a shop in the West End of London, and Mannering owns it. That's only one of the things he does! You might think I'm a fair performer as a private eye, but Mannering—" he chuckled. "The thing about Mannering is that he'll only work for love. I don't mean what you mean!" he added hurriedly, seeing the way her expression changed. "Or else because he's a personal angle in a case, and he has in this. He sold the diamonds to Wannaker, which gives him sentimental interest in them now. He doesn't like his best customers to be robbed, or American visitors to England being treated nastily." Stocker was only half serious. "Beginning to understand?"

Helen went to her bag.

"It's a slow beginning." She opened the bag, and

then remembered that she had emptied her last pack of Pall Mall on the bus. Stocker was proffering his thick silver case. "Very slow," she said. "Thank you."

They lit up.

"I'll try again," Stocker said equably. "I saw your brother Robbie, when making inquiries. He said he'd been framed. Then he vanished – after telling you about me and his troubles, I imagine."

That was a shrewd guess, but Helen was quick to deny it.

"He didn't. I learned about the diamonds afterwards, Robbie didn't tell me. I found your name – the Agency's name, in a pocket of a coat of Robbie's. These people told me the rest, said they could prove that Robbie stole the diamonds." She burst out, "*Can* they?"

"Mannering has quite a reputation," Stocker told her, "especially among jewel thieves. He can get to places which Scotland Yard doesn't know about, and pick up information a copper wouldn't hear in a life time. He had a scrap – fight to you – with this mob six months or so ago, and some of them are still Her Majesty's guests. Once you've had the raw edge of John Mannering, you remember it. There are times when I'm nervous of him myself." He gave that quick, enheartening grin. "But don't worry, he won't bite you. You'll be pleasantly surprised. He – "

"What will he do if Robbie did take those diamonds?" Helen asked.

Stocker said gently: "Haven't you any faith, Miss Chadwick?"

The question shook her and she didn't answer. Stocker moved about the room, looking at the shabby furniture and the worn carpet, at the few oddments of hers that she had here; the expensive baggage, the good quality clothes and expensive make up accessories.

"I want you to meet Mannering soon," he said. "Have you any objection?"

"No," Helen told him. "I don't think I have."

"That's fine," said Stocker, lightly. "Let me give you one piece of advice, then. Tell Mannering the truth. If there's anything you don't want to tell him, keep it back but don't lie. If he thought you were taking him for a ride, he'd lose interest, and drop you just like that." Stocker snapped his fingers, making her start. He grinned. "See what I mean?"

"Yes," Helen said.

"I'll fix a meeting," Stocker said. "You stay here."

.    .    .

It was easy to be patient at first. Now and again Helen looked out of the window, but no one was watching the hotel, or watching her. At least, she could see no one whom she recognised. The elation hadn't gone completely. The build-up which the fresh-faced man had given Mannering couldn't be entirely without foundation. She had an ally, who had good, practical reasons for being on her side.

She took off the little white hat, then unpinned her hair. She had this plaited and coiled at the back, thick, corn-coloured, the colour one would expect with her blue eyes. With the plaits hanging down her back, she looked younger, almost starry-eyed; that was with relief, or with hope. She didn't know which, and she didn't greatly care. She had never made a habit of being precise about her emotions. She had lived carelessly, like Robbie. Not really foolishly; carelessly.

Looking at herself in the mirror, she was calm enough to indulge in a few minutes of self-analysis. They did not go deep, but they were deeper than any she had been moved to try before. Life had been easy, too easy, for both of them. There had been plenty of money — not a fortune but always enough; and there had been little supervision since High School days, when their parents had died. That had happened so long ago that it was hardly a thing to sorrow about, one regretted it vaguely, impersonally, although now and again a moment of poignancy stabbed and hurt. Not often and not much.

Glenton, New Jersey . . . a white-painted frame house just beyond the city limits of the little town . . . a tiny river, running through the apple orchard . . . grass lawns littered in the Fall with the small brown and gold leaves of beech and birch . . . an indulgent widowed Uncle, a beaming, sunny-tempered black cook-general, an over-indulgent black chauffeur . . . she had had all of these things, and so had Robbie.

There had been friends, too; the clubs; a car each; New York was only an hour's drive away, with everything, just everything, from the Stork Club and the Waldorf-Astoria to honky-tonks and clip-joints. Greenwich Village had appealed, until its false Bohemia palled; oh, *every*thing. There had been boy-friends, of course, but somehow 'friends' was all. At times, she thought that she was cold; that passion was a thing she would never know. 'Boys' were all hands, awkwardness, embarrassment or over-boldness. For some reason which she couldn't understand, most men kept away from her. Middle-aged Romeos with an exciting reputation among her girl-friends never approached her, except nicely. It was as if there were two worlds, and she lived in one remote from most of her friends so far as *that* was concerned.

Sometimes she had asked herself why. Was it her tall, rangy figure? Her striking eyes? Did she repel men? There was nothing the matter with her figure, was there? But she seldom thought like that, and now she was thinking about the ease of the past life, not its minor puzzles. There had been no difficulties until

Robbie had left for England. She hadn't wanted him to, but he had come back from his Military Service restless and unsettled, and beaten fierce competition for the job with Wannaker, as secretary and general factotum. It was all very pleasant, for Wannaker was a middle-aged millionaire – shoes – and was travelling with his young wife.

The next she had heard was an urgent cable; could she come to London?

The mystery, the fear, the shadows, had come upon her very quickly after that. She had seen Robbie and been horrified; he was tearful, tense, terrified, but said only that he'd been fired. Later, she had found out why. Then Ben had told her that Wannaker thought that Robbie had been the thief, but wouldn't name him to the police out of a sense of loyalty. 'Ben' would – if he didn't get the 'ice'.

Robbie had been living in a boarding house near Kensington High Street, fearful of the things he had not told her about. Then he had disappeared. Next, the three men had started to talk to her, to threaten, to fill her mind with the shadow of menace.

She was almost out of money, too. She had airmailed to Glenton for some, and it hadn't arrived; but money had been the least of her worries, Robbie the greatest. Now there was the brisk, bright Stocker who had not told her everything he knew, and talk of Mannering, and –

The telephone bell rang.

For the first time for four days she answered it without a spasm of nervous fear.

"Helen," a man said. The voice of the short, stout Ben froze her again. "Helen," he repeated, "you keep away from Mannering. Understand? You keep away from him."

31

# 4

## OUT OF THE BLUE

ALL Helen's fears came back, and they were stronger than ever. There was nothing that Ben would not do; or dare. His threat was explicit, the order had to be obeyed because of what he might, he could, do to Robbie.

She must keep away from Mannering.

"You'll be watched all the time," Ben went on, "and if you see Mannering, then brother Robbie – " he stopped at that, as if he knew quite well what thought would flash through her mind. "And listen. Stay where you are tonight, don't come to us. Just wait until you get your orders."

She didn't answer.

"You still there?" Ben's voice was higher-pitched.

"Y-yes. Yes, I'm here."

"Don't have anything to do with Mannering, and stay where you are until you hear from us," Ben said. "Don't come out tonight. And listen – don't tell Mannering or Stocker or anyone where you were to meet us." He paused, then went on with hoarse emphasis: "Got that all clear, Helen, honey?"

"Sure, I – I understand."

"Mind you do what I say," Ben said. "You ever *seen* a man without a nose?"

He rang off.

Helen put the receiver down slowly. Her forehead, her upper lip and the palms of her hands were damp with sweat. She felt hot and cold in turn, and shivered much more than she had all day. She did not realise how much of this was nervous reaction to shock and disappointment, because she had known hope and had it snatched away from her. It seemed that Ben was all-seeing and omnipotent; and because he knew where Robbie was, she had to obey his orders.

It was quiet and lonely, and the brisk confidence of Stocker was like a reluctantly forgotten dream, only the beauty of which lingered. She moved about the room, slowly, distractedly, moving things. She kept seeing pictures of Robbie in her mind's eye. Robbie, fishing in a big pond where there was a big snappy turtle; Robbie, playing baseball; Robbie, laughing — Robbie doing all the things a boy should do. And Robbie without a nose. He was handsome; more handsome than she was lovely, he had the looks of the family. The very thought of the threatened disfigurement was enough to curdle her blood.

It was difficult to think.

If Mannering came here, what should she do? The hotel was being watched, after all; Ben hadn't said so but he had made it clear that she couldn't do a thing without him knowing. If Stocker came back or if he telephoned or Mannering telephoned, what should she do?

She walked about the room for twenty minutes, and her fears stirred in her like yeast leavening dough. Then came a sharp tap at her door, when she had heard no one approaching; it set her heart thudding and racing.

"Who — who is it?"

"Hall porter, Miss Chadwick."

How did she know that was true? She didn't recognise the voice, but she had hardly seen the hall porter, and she wouldn't recognise him. It might be Ben or Dan or the youth or a colleague. Moistening her lips in a way which had become familiar, she went to the door and opened it cautiously.

"Letter for you, Miss Chadwick," said a middle-aged man in some kind of uniform with red braid. He was just a porter, with a letter stretched out towards her. He smiled. "Just delivered, by hand," he said. "It's marked urgent."

It was; in black ink.

"Thank you very much."

"It's a pleasure, Miss Chadwick." Why did he utter her name at every opportunity?

He smiled, saluted, and turned smartly away. She closed the door and looked at the envelope, addressed in a bold handwriting to her, and with the *Urgent* heavily underlined. She hesitated before she began to open it, and her heart was in her mouth.

She unfolded the note, and then almost screamed. It was in Robbie's writing; unmistakably his:

> "Sis, they're devils, do what they say.
> Will you, Sis? They're *devils*."

.　　.　　.

It was eight o'clock.

Helen had had dinner in her room, because she was so nervous, and did not know how literally to take Ben's orders. She had heard nothing more from Stocker, was already beginning to believe that he would fail her, that everything he had said had been a pose; and yet the name of Mannering *had* frightened Percy Morino.

She had sent for some cigarettes, a packet of twenty, and half were gone.

She felt that she needed a whisky, but was afraid that if she started drinking she would want to go on. It was a fear which had been in her since her childhood when a drunken neighbour who had killed herself had been held up as an awful example. Drink could kill, could warp the mind – and so she had always been cautious about hard liquor. But she needed Dutch courage now.

She heard footsteps in the passage, a woman's; two or three people had passed, so this might have nothing to do with her; but it might. Her heart came to her throat again, and for a moment she felt that she could not breathe.

There was a tap.

She stood up, stiffly, cold again, a cigarette shaking in her hand.

"What is it?"

"Can you spare me a minute, Miss Chadwick?" It was a woman, and she sounded young.

Helen pulled back the bolt, unfastened the chain, and then pulled back the catch and opened the door very slowly. Only a woman stood there, though; a woman of about her own build, with a well-developed bust and with a big hat which covered all her hair, and hid part of her face; but she smiled, and Helen saw and liked that.

"May I come in?"

"Please do." Helen stood aside, and then closed the door.

"Bolt, chain *and* key," remarked the other woman. "You're really nervous, aren't you? You needn't be, you know, with John Mannering cheering for you. That *is* the right phrase, isn't it? Cheering for you?"

She smiled, and showed that she was nice-looking, fair-complexioned and, now that she was in better light, fair-haired. As if to draw attention to this, she took off her hat with a careless gesture, and let it drop on to the bed. Then she poked her fingers through her thick hair. She had something of the confidence of the man Stocker.

"We could almost be twins, couldn't we?" she remarked.

*"Twins?"*

"Yes," the girl said, and then rested a cool hand lightly on Helen's arm. "I'm sorry, I shouldn't keep

35

you in suspense. I'm May Sharp, and I'm working for Mannering – that is, I've been hired out to him, because Pip Stocker says I'm like you." She smiled quickly, brightly. "Don't I wish I had your eyes!"

"I don't understand," Helen said, but she was beginning to breathe more fiercely.

"Why, it's simple! After dark, you're to leave the hotel by the back way, and I shall stay here until you come back. If anyone calls up – Ben, for instance – I can answer. I'm not so bad at voices. Listen: 'No, I just can't do it, I can't do it. But don't hurt Robbie, you understand, don't hurt Robbie'."

Helen backed to a chair.

"Why, that's just how I would talk!"

"That's what I'm hoping," May Sharp said happily. "Listen, Helen, when you get out the back way, a man will be waiting for you, and he'll take you to Mannering. I've just one piece of advice – don't lie to Mannering."

She was echoing Stocker.

"I don't have to lie," Helen said. "I *don't* lie."

May Sharp laughed. "That makes you more of an angel than I'll ever be!" She opened her bag and proffered cigarettes from a plastic case with a lighter fitted at one end. "That was a present from a friend in New York, ain't it cute?" She laughed, and lapsed into her normal English accent. "We know that Ben telephoned you, we had an in with the telephone operator here. Don't worry – don't worry at all. The other side's scared, you know."

.     .     .

Was *Ben* scared?

Helen could imagine that lanky Dan wouldn't have much nerve, under pressure; and she knew that young

36

Percy Morino was a coward, in spite of his bombast; but Ben?

Was he really scared?

.       .       .

May Sharp looked at her watch an hour later, and then stood up from the chair; but she was careful to keep away from the window; she had been careful to make sure that two shadows couldn't appear at the window at the same moment, because she knew that the hotel was watched.

"It's time," she said, "I'll keep my fingers crossed for you."

"I – I expect it'll be all right," Helen said, and did not know how quavery her voice was.

"Oh, you'll get away from here," said May calmly. "I mean, good luck with John Mannering. I think it will be all right, those eyes should win him over, even if the rest of you doesn't impress him!" She went with Helen to the door, holding her arm tightly. "He's the most handsome man you've ever seen. Hollywood folk would rave over him."

"Would – they?"

"Yes," said May, and went on slowly, thoughtfully: "He's tremendous. Did you ever meet a man who really belonged to yesterday? Who ought to wear a periwig and flash a sword out of his scabbard – that kind of man? He's like that, sometimes. And at others he's just a cold fish." She laughed. "Not often, though."

She opened the door, and looked out, as if to make sure that no one watched. She moved back.

"All clear. God bless."

Helen didn't speak, but stepped into the dimly lighted passage. No one was there. She went slowly towards the head of the stairs, and then went up, not down; May had told her exactly what to do. She went to the next floor along a passage which narrowed near a second landing, then down a flight of narrow stairs. These brought her out into a hallway near the kitchen. The kitchen door was open and she could see the stainless steel sink, and smell cooking.

A few yards further, and she was at the back door. She opened it.

The night was dark but for the stars. A cool wind blew along a narrow street, and it may have been that which made her shiver. She had to turn right, and would be met at the corner. She didn't know by whom. She wished that someone had come with her, that she needn't be alone even for a few minutes.

She reached the corner.

Stocker stood beneath a street lamp by a small car which had its side lights on.

"Okay," he said, moving swiftly towards her, and her heart began to beat very fast again, threatening to choke her. He took her arm; his grip was very firm. "All clear." He opened the car door, and helped her in, then hurried towards the other side, climbed in, slammed the door, and started the engine. He seemed to do everything in one swinging movement. They swung away from the kerb and into the road towards the corner of a well-lit street.

Helen sat back, holding her breath.

She was going to see Mannering. Ben had been fooled. If he hadn't been fooled, then Robbie —

They turned the corner.

Helen looked round, and saw a car parked outside the hotel; it began to move after them, and was on their heels at the next corner.

"We — we're being followed," she gasped. "Look."

# 5

# A MAN FROM HOME

"DON'T worry," Stocker said, "we'll shake 'em off."

He turned a corner, and the other car followed.

"Maybe we will," Helen said, "but that — that isn't the point, we — we didn't want them to know that I was leaving did we?"

"They're good," conceded Stocker. "They're very good." He put his foot down and they went fast; but whenever Helen turned her head, she could see the lights of the other car, the only one behind them.

These were narrow streets, poorly lit although so close to Oxford Street. Helen did not think of that or of anything except the car which kept so close behind and the failure of the manœuvre. It seemed as if failure had become part of her life.

"Hold tight," Stocker said, casually.

Next moment, he swung the wheel and they turned a corner with the tyres squealing, roared along with headlights blazing, then turned left — left again — right — right. It made Helen dizzy. One moment she was thrown against the door, the next a swerve took her against Stocker. The odd, almost the alarming thing was that he was whistling softly — something from *Guys and Dolls*.

He slowed down.

The car behind them had disappeared.

"We'll be all right now," said Stocker. "Don't get so tense, Miss Chadwick, you're on the winning side."

She didn't speak.

"Cigarette," he offered, and held out the big case, holding the wheel with one hand until both cigarettes were alight. "If you keep your head, do what Mannering tells you and tell him the truth and nothing but the truth, you'll be fine. You won't have a thing to worry about," he finished, and then after a few seconds, declared: "We're here."

He turned into a narrow street, and stopped outside a shop. She got out. Lamplight shone on the empty window of the shop, and on the deep fascia board with gilt lettering boasting the legend:

QUINNS

She got out, long legs moving swiftly. Stocker came round and joined her, put a hand on her arm, and led the way to the door. Shadowy figures moved inside the shop. She felt as frightened as she had when Ben and the others had been after her.

"I'll see you later," Stocker said. "Good luck."

A tall man with silvery grey hair opened the door.

"This way, Madam," he said, in one of those subdued English voices which always seem to belong to the films but actually belonged here in London. "Mr Mannering has been delayed, but Mr Wannaker is here."

.        .        .

Helen followed the silvery-haired man along the gloomy lengths of the shop, then up a narrow flight of twisting stairs. She had to duck, or she would have banged her head on oak beams which stood out from the ceiling. The courteous guide kept murmuring "Be careful here, please." There was a half landing, then a full landing; and every tread was worn hollow with the feet of people over the centuries. But she was not conscious of the age of the place or the manners of the man.

*Wannaker* was here.

If Ben were right, Robbie had robbed Wannaker.

She didn't know him, except by photograph and reputation. It was a good reputation, so far as it went; and she liked his television programme, *The Wannaker Wonders Walking the World in Wannaker Shoes*. She didn't want to see Wannaker, she wanted to see Mannering — or anyone who would help her to get Robbie free without being injured or disfigured.

The silvery-haired man stopped, tapped on a door, and opened it on an unmistakably American: "Come in."

"Miss Helen Chadwick," the man murmured: as a Hollywood butler would murmur. He stood by the open door, tall and impressive, bowing slightly as Helen passed him. She had to, because she could hardly draw back. She was filled with uncertainty and embarrassment; what could she say to a man who believed that her brother had robbed him of a fortune in precious stones?

A tall, good-looking, fair-haired man in the late twenties or early thirties, certainly not the Wannaker she expected, stood in a small room. He smiled a welcome.

"Hi, Miss Chadwick." He moved, with his hand outstretched. "I'm Jeff Wannaker, and I'm delighted to know you."

His handclasp was cool, firm, friendly; so was his smile. He had nice eyes and wrinkles at the corners, which half suggested that he was older than she had thought at first. He was handsome in a Scandinavian way, with very fair hair and eyebrows, rather large features and grey eyes.

"Why, hallo," Helen said, weakly. "I expected — "

"My Dad," Jeff Wannaker finished for her. "I can imagine that, but Dad won't be here tonight, unless John Mannering's changed his plans. Just you and me and John." His smile had a warm friendliness which did more than anything else to make Helen feel that life could be good, and that there were real reasons for hope. "Let me get you a drink," Wannaker offered, and turned to an array of bottles standing inside a small corner cupboard just behind him.

It was an unusual room, odd-shaped, long and narrow except at one end, where it widened, making a long T shape. The ceiling was low. The walls were panelled, and some small oil paintings, all heads and shoulders, with richness and splendour in the colouring and the medieval subjects, hung on them. The brown carpet was very thick, the furniture all old and unfamiliar – the wood seemed almost black with age. An electric fire burned with a bright reflector behind it. Helen felt the warmth on her feet and legs as she sat down.

"What will you drink?" Wannaker asked. "Martini, Manhattan, Scotch-and-soda or even on the rocks? This Mannering's civilised!"

"I'll have – oh, anything."

"That suggests you don't get much practice," said Wannaker dryly. "I'll mix you a dry Martini like you've never had in your life before. Will it do you good!" He winked and snapped his fingers, then busied himself with the bottles and glasses. She relaxed. The fire was soothing, the room was pleasing, but would Jeff Wannaker behave like this if he knew that Robbie was suspected of having stolen his father's jewels? She wondered why she was so surprised to find that Wannaker had a son of this age; that was probably because Wannaker was young-looking himself, according to his photographs, and also according to Robbie.

She lit a cigarette.

Jeff turned round, with the drinks. He looked down at her, for a second or two, still smiling. It was an intimate kind of look. There was a kind of friendly amusement in his eyes; a brother-to-kid-sister kind of look, she could remember having seen it in Robbie before now.

She took the drink.

"Here's to getting better acquainted," he said, "and to the most startling eyes in the world! Did anyone ever tell you about those eyes?"

"Listen — "

"I know, I know," he said, "you're not in the mood for airy compliments, only that wasn't airy. But let's drink to our better acquaintance, your eyes can come later." He drank. "You just can't wait for Mannering, can you?" he drawled.

"I'm very anxious to see him."

"You won't be disappointed," Wannaker promised, and chuckled. "I'd got such a build-up I couldn't believe that the man lived who could justify it, but I don't argue now, I just believe it. What do you know about John?"

"Practically nothing. Mr Stocker told me a little, that's all."

"These British," Jeff scoffed, "they don't even talk about their friends, it's considered immodest. Dad and I were told about John Mannering by a friend — a *Chicago Sun* ace, who wouldn't be easily fooled. It seems that Mannering owns this shop, Quinns, and it's world famous. He's a connoisseur of precious stones, antiques, *objets d'art,* old masters, anything you like. Like he was born to it," added Jeff with that broad and attractive grin. "There isn't a dealer in the world from New York to Berlin and Los Angeles to Moscow who wouldn't take Mannering's word on values. And that's only part of it."

Helen finished her drink. It warmed her spirit as well as her blood. Jeff Wannaker's enthusiasm cheered her up, too. Suddenly, there was no need to fear the immediate disaster, and gradually she thawed, so that she could see other things besides a disfigured Robbie.

"They swear that there isn't a private eye in England like him," declared Jeff. "No, ma'am, he even gets

consulted by Scotland Yard on jewel cases, but they
don't like him all that — because if he thinks they're
after the wrong man, he says so." Jeff chuckled again,
obviously determined to put her at her ease. "He hunts
the bad men his own way, and it's just too bad if the
police don't like his way."

She felt like echoing: "Bad men." And the brief rest
from worry was gone.

"Have another Martini," Jeff said, and took her
glass. "Don't worry, Helen, just take it easy."

She wished he would say something about Robbie.

He didn't, but went on talking about Mannering and
his reputation. It was easy to believe him when he said
that he would never have believed that a man could
live up to it. But she was only half listening, now —
wondering why he was so friendly, how much he knew,
whether Mannering was working for Wannaker Senior
and therefore *hunting* Robbie. Could she be wanted to
help to betray Robbie? Was that why Mannering offered
her help, and why Jeff Wannaker was so amiable?

"There's a painting of John," Wannaker said, and
pointed to one of the oils.

Then she knew he was ribbing her.

The portrait he pointed to was of a Cavalier, *circa*
the seventeenth century. He wore a plumed hat, the
bright coat, the wig of the period. He was a handsome
beggar, with gleaming brown eyes and a kind of half
smile which didn't reveal his teeth but suggested that
at any moment he would break into a laugh. He had a
black moustache, close-clipped, not at all like the long
moustaches of the period. His face was tanned, and he
looked hardy — as if the very spirit of his times were
in him, and he could swagger through the salons or
coffee houses of the time, taking his women where he
fancied; or he could walk through the narrow streets of
London, keen-edged rapier sheathed but ready to flash
into action if thieves and vagabonds attacked. It was

44

easy to imagine him a man who would risk his life to help a fugitive Prince to safety, or would duel to the death to defend a woman's honour or his own good name. A man who would gladly look for trouble.

The strange, the compelling thing was that thoughts like that – not so detailed nor so full, but like it – passed through her mind, although she knew that Wannaker had been teasing her. She wasn't angry; the spirit had gone from her.

"You don't believe me," Jeff said, "but – "

The door opened, and the man of the painting came in.

He was dressed in a navy blue suit, like any well-dressed man in London, his black hair was cut short, his moustache – it was the moustache of the painting, too.

Helen knew that she was gaping, but couldn't stop.

It wasn't only at the face, which was the image of the Cavalier's; it was at the man himself, the way he moved, the cool assurance, the almost fascinating movement of hands, of eyes, of lips. He smiled, in exactly the same way as the Cavalier was smiling, as if only good manners kept him from bursting into laughter.

He closed the door.

"Hi, John," said Jeff Wannaker, "Helen can hardly wait to say hallo."

Helen stood up, slowly.

Mannering came towards her, hand outstretched, the smile somehow different; just for her. It was as if Jeff Wannaker had disappeared, and did not exist. Mannering's eyes held hers; hazel eyes with a great light in them, and an abiding confidence. She had been terrified; but she felt that she would know a security, now, which she had never known since the bad news had come from Robbie.

They shook hands.

Mannering said lightly: "I'm sorry I'm late, and delighted to see you, Helen." He used her name as freely, as naturally, as any American would have done, but his deep voice was like something which had sprung from the traditions of a thousand years. "I'm sorry we've had to use all this cloak-and-dagger stuff, too, but I think we'll be glad before we've finished." He turned to the corner cupboard and poured himself a drink. "Here's to confounding the bad men," he added, and then said in the same assured voice: "And I don't mean Robbie, even if he were fool enough to take the jewels. Did he take them, Helen?"

6

## MANNERING SUGGESTS

HELEN did not say 'no'.

She understood, in that moment, why Stocker had warned her not to lie to Mannering. Lying would do no good because he would know, or at least he would sense, that he hadn't been told the truth; and she could well believe that once she lied, he would lose interest in her.

"I don't know," she said, "I just can't believe that he did."

"Didn't he tell you all about it? No confession?"

"No. He was — he was worried about something, said there was trouble and that he'd been fired, but he didn't get around to saying why."

"I see," said Mannering. "In its way that's a pity, but at least it means we can still keep an open mind." He said that to Jeff Wannaker more than to Helen, as

46

if he wanted Jeff back in their counsels. "What else did he tell you?"

She told Mannering all that she could, but it wasn't much. Then, prompted gently, she told him about the first meeting with Ben, when Ben had sidled up alongside her in the street and started whispering; and seemed to have been whispering ever since, with those threats and menaces and tales of horror.

"So Ben thinks that Robbie stole the diamonds and handed them to you to hide," Mannering said, as if the notion were something to be laughed at.

"Oh, yes, there's no doubt he thinks that."

"He must have a reason," Mannering remarked easily, "and the problem is to find out what put the idea into his head. Or one problem is." He lit a cigarette and sat on the corner of a small table. It was difficult not to look from him to the picture and back again; it *was* the same man. "We have to prise the truth out of Ben and his parcel of hoodlums." He looked at Helen, as if he were fascinated by her eyes. "What matters most to you, Helen?"

"Helping Robbie."

Mannering smiled faintly.

"The reports I have about your brother are that he's young, impulsive and selfish, but not a criminal type."

"Of course he's not!"

"If he stole the jewels, it was probably because someone else put him up to it," Mannering said calmly. "He wouldn't be likely to take them for himself. Any fascinating blonde in his young life?"

"I don't think so."

"Not back home, you mean," Jeff broke in. It wasn't exactly that he felt as if he had been shouldered out of the conversation; rather that here was a moment when he could help her. He watched her very closely.

"I didn't hear of him meeting a girl over here," said Helen. "I wish—"

47

"Say just what's in your mind," encouraged Mannering.

"I wish I could see the whole picture," Helen said abruptly. "Everyone shows me a little piece, but that's all."

"Fair enough," conceded Mannering. "Except that none of us knows what the whole picture's like. Still, we do know more of it than you. The jewels are Mrs Wannaker's and worth about twenty-five thousand pounds, and were stolen three weeks ago. That was just after Robbie had been fired—"

*"After?"* breathed Helen.

"Yes."

"Ben made me think—" Helen stopped abruptly, confused by the news. "But why was he fired?"

Jeff said rather too quickly: "We don't rightly know, but Dad doesn't always have to have a reason. He's hot tempered, and if Robbie didn't please Dad or Elaine over something, he'd be fired."

Helen didn't speak, but thought: 'or Elaine'. That was Wannaker's new wife, she knew. Jeff's stepmother.

"Robbie left Mr Wannaker on a Friday," Mannering said, "and the jewels were stolen on the Saturday. The police were called in at once. A thief clumsy enough to be an amateur had forced the lock of the apartment door, and also the bedroom door, but the thief had a key to the jewel box. It wasn't so careless as it seemed, there was a special case with a false compartment, steel lined, almost as good as a safe," Mannering went on. "The fact that the thief had a key suggested that it was someone who knew all about that case. Robbie could easily have had a key made —until he left the job, he had one."

"Did—Robbie keep it?" Helen asked huskily.

"Yes, but we won't jump to conclusions. The police questioned your brother, but didn't hold him. His room was searched, and nothing found to point a finger of guilt. A week later, he vanished."

"We know they kidnapped him," Helen said quickly.

"It looks like that," Mannering agreed. "But he wasn't wanted by Scotland Yard, Helen, and no one went to much trouble to look for him. Except you." He paused, to offer cigarettes and light them. He went back to the table and sat on it, calm, thoughtful, yet somehow less arresting than when she had first seen him. Perhaps because she was getting used to him, or else because she was so tensely interested in his story. "That's one angle we can see. The other is Saul Wannaker's. He asked me to help him find the jewels. Stocker was busy for the insurance company by then, so we worked together. In looking for Robbie we found you — and then it came out that Ben and his friend were worrying you. Ben is bad," went on Mannering, and paused as if what he were going to say next was of compelling importance. He even lowered his voice: "But the man whom Ben works for is corruption itself."

That was all.

Helen felt herself shiver.

"And arising out of all this," Mannering went on, very softly, "is the fact we talked of first — that Ben and the man he works for appear to believe that Robbie stole the diamonds. And they've kidnapped Robbie, hoping to make him talk — or to make you talk." He gave the smile of the portrait again. "He must be tough!"

"Tough." That surprised her. "Why?"

"If he hasn't told them where the diamonds are, obviously he must be," Mannering said. "Either very tough or innocent."

*Was* Robbie tough?

Mannering and Jeff Wannaker were watching Helen

closely, as if they hoped to learn something from her expression. She looked from one to the other. She didn't believe that Robbie was so tough that he could withstand torture or ill-treatment, so – he must be innocent.

She stood up, impatience putting fire into her words.

"Can you find him? Are you looking for him? Have you done anything to help?"

Mannering said mildly: "Not much, yet, but there hasn't been a lot of time. We've already started worrying Ben and his mob. You've run up against one of the two dangerous gangs in London," he added lightly but emphatically. "There are only the two."

Helen didn't speak.

"I heard from Pip Stocker that they tried to scare you off," Mannering went on. "They'd prefer not to have to deal with me, but they can't have it all their own way, can they?" His eyes gleamed, as if he could see the need for battle and was longing to start. "Helen – where were you to meet these men tonight?"

"At Piccadilly Circus."

"In the street?"

"Yes!"

Mannering was obviously disappointed, but went on almost without a pause: "Have they talked about anything else?"

Helen said: "I – I don't understand you. They've threatened . . ."

"I mean, about anything besides diamonds?"

She looked and felt bewildered.

"Why, no."

"Have they suggested that Robbie stole anything else?"

She exclaimed: "No! No, they didn't, I don't understand you. What else would there be?"

Mannering didn't answer, but seemed more satisfied; and she realised suddenly how forceful his questions had been.

"All right," Mannering said at last, speaking more easily. "I had to find out. There's something else missing and I need to know whether these three realise it. They'll be at you again — and when they come, try to find out if they're thinking only of diamonds."

Helen said: "What — what else would they talk about?"

"We don't want you to know," Mannering said.

Helen looked from him to Wannaker; then suddenly she felt *mad*. It was a climax to bewilderment and fear, brought on by his calm: "They'll be at you again." It was as if these two men, handsome and so self-assured, were using her as bait. They talked in half-truths, hinting here, insinuating there. Although it was chiefly at Mannering, the flare of anger also spread to Jeff.

She felt the blood rush to her cheeks. She knew that her eyes sparkled. She knew that her hands clenched and that she was straining herself to her full height. She did not know that she looked magnificent.

"What is the matter with you?" she demanded, and her voice was low-pitched, she fought for self-control. "Why are you trying to make a fool out of me? What are you saying? Are you calling me a liar?"

Mannering said gently:

"I'd lose a bet if you were. No, Helen, our money's on you. Something else was missing. We don't know whether there were two separate thieves or just one. Finding out is very important, to Robbie as well as to others. We'll protect you, but we want you to try to find out if these men think you can lead them to anything else."

"It really matters," Jeff put in.

Helen said: "Well, I guess you know what you're talking about. I'll try." She shivered again. "But I hoped I wouldn't see Ben and the others again."

"It won't last much longer," Mannering promised. "Remember that in a lot of ways the other thing's

51

more important – even than danger to Robbie, even than danger to you.''

The strange thing was that she believed him.

## 7

## MAY SHARP

"You'll do a fine job,'' Jeff Wannaker said, "I'm positive about that, Helen, but if you change your mind, and don't feel you can face Ben any more, tell Mannering. I want you to promise me that.''

"I won't change my mind,'' she said.

"In case you do, promise me.''

"If I change my mind,'' Helen said, "I'll tell Mannering. I'll call him at the number he gave me.''

She had a note of the number in her bag.

"That's fine,'' Jeff said. "That's fine.''

He stopped the car at a corner near her hotel. She could see the red glow from the neon hotel sign, just round the corner. It was an hour or more since she had been to the shop; half-an-hour since she had last seen Mannering. In some odd way, he still seemed to be with her – a third party to her and Jeff.

Jeff had driven her back.

Now, he got out of the car, handed her out, stood very near her for a moment, embarrassingly close. She felt as she had felt often before, that she could never really warm to a man, never know passion. Yet he was – very handsome, distinguished; the light of a street lamp told her all that.

"You can trust Mannering,'' Jeff said, "he won't let any harm come to you. Or to Robbie. And if you couldn't trust Mannering, you could trust me.''

She made herself say: "Yes, I know."

He squeezed her arm.

"Good luck."

She turned and walked hurriedly towards the back entrance, knowing just which way to go. No one followed her, no one appeared to be watching, except Jeff. She was very conscious of the pressure of his fingers on her arm, and the closeness of his body, and of his good looks. Something like excitement stirred in her, but that was forgotten when she reached the hotel, and a man appeared.

He stared.

"Good-night, Miss Chadwick." It was the hall-porter.

"Good-night."

She went in, passed the kitchen, and went up the secondary stairs. The hotel was very quiet. She reached her landing, and walked along quickly, but her foot-steps slackened as she reached her own room. She stood outside it for a moment. Light showed at the sides of the door. May Sharp would be inside, waiting for her. May would tell her if Ben or anyone else had called, whether there was anything she ought to know.

She tapped; it felt odd, tapping at her own door.

The other woman didn't answer.

Helen frowned, and tapped again, more sharply. There was still no answer.

Anxiety came storming back – and then it thawed out again as she reasoned with herself, argued that there was now no need to fear. May had gone along to the bathroom, or gone to get some cigarettes, or . . .

She tapped again.

Nothing happened.

She tried the door, and it opened; the catch wasn't down. The light inside shone very brightly as she pushed the door open wider. Something caught at her nerves, like a hand clutching at her. She was afraid of

53

what she might find, frightened to go in. Her breath came in short, sharp gasps.

"Don't be a coward!" she exclaimed aloud, and thrust the door back and strode in.

May Sharp lay on the bed, with her throat cut. The pillows and sheets were soaked in the hideous red of blood.

.     .     .

Helen stood there, as if flesh and blood had turned to stone; staring. The corn-coloured hair, so like her own, was spread out on the pillow, glinting in the electric light. May's face was turned towards the door. Her mouth was slack, her eyes partly open, and glazed – but only the throat was hideous. One arm hung over the side of the bed, the other was lying lightly on her breast. Her legs were drawn up, quite naturally; the shoes were on the bed. She looked almost natural, too, if one could forget the gash.

Helen moved a step forward.

It was like stepping from one life into another.

Blood flowed back into her veins. She was cooler than she had been for some time. She understood the dread significance of this: May Sharp had been killed in mistake for her. She felt quite sure of that as she went nearer. By the time she reached the bed, she knew that she had to make sure that the other woman was dead.

What ought she to do?

It was pointless to feel for the pulse; or to hope.

She went to the telephone, and her fingers were cold as she dialled the number which Mannering had given her, one she was to use in emergency. She recognised Mannering's voice.

"This is Helen Chadwick," she said, and her voice sounded a long way off.

"Yes, Helen?" Mannering said, without surprise.

"You — you must come to the hotel, straight away." She could hardly get the words out.

"Why?"

"May Sharp is — " Helen stopped, as her breath seemed to come so fast that it would choke her. "May Sharp is — "

"Wait there," Mannering said in a sharper voice. "I'll come at once."

.        .        .

Helen opened the door to Mannering, and he came in and glanced at the bed, then at her. He looked capable of fighting the world. He took her arm and made her sit down, drew a silver flask from his hip pocket and said:

"Have a nip of this, it'll do you good."

Then he went to the bed.

He did not hurry, and she wanted to scream at him, tell him not to waste time looking about the room. He turned away at last, and she hadn't sipped the brandy in the flask. He moved across, and made her.

"I don't get it," Mannering said at last, and he was no longer smiling, no longer the Cavalier ready to break into a brilliant smile. "I just don't get it." He was looking at her steadily. "Why should they want to kill — "

"Me," she said, chokily.

"All right," he conceded, "why should they want to kill you? Or did they know — " he ran a hand across his forehead. She felt empty, disappointed, hopeless, helpless. He wasn't anything like he had been made out to be. This crime bewildered him, he didn't know what to do.

He swung round, swiftly, silently, with almost magical ease of movement.

She remembered Stocker moving like that but without the superb ease.

He stepped towards the door, with his hand at his pocket, and she was quite sure that he had a gun. The handle of the door moved. He reached it, hand stretched out to clasp it and pull the door open.

Then Helen heard a movement from the wardrobe. She swung round, and saw a man with a gun. She screamed on a stifled note as she saw Mannering move with bewildering, suffocating speed. He seemed to fly across the room, she heard a hissing sound, saw the man by the wardrobe stagger and his gun droop. He hadn't fired — and now Mannering was like a fury, reaching him, smashing at him, tearing the scarf from his face.

It was Lanky Dan.

In that moment, Helen truly expected miracles; but the kind she wanted didn't come. Mannering drew back from Lanky Dan, there seemed nothing to fear — and then Percy Morino spoke from the door.

Mannering turned swiftly.

Lanky Dan struck Mannering's gun out of his grasp, kicked his legs from under him and pushed him against the wall. Mannering was defeated; just like that.

There was silence; a stifled quiet. It was as if the two men could not believe in their own success. Then Morino moved his gun towards Mannering, and said:

"We — we've got to put him away. We can't — leave him alive, we — "

"No!" The half-uttered threat terrified Helen.

Mannering didn't speak or move.

"*He* can't help you," Morino said, while Lanky Dan moved. "He won't be able to help you or anyone else again."

Mannering spoke for the first time.

"I thought Dizzy wanted the Wannaker jewels," he said, and smiled at some secret joke. *Smiled*.

.     .     .

They were the last words Helen heard that night.

A movement from Morino made her turn round, her lips opening in the beginning of a scream. Then a cloth, soft and warm, closed about her mouth and covered her eyes. She did scream, but the sound was muffled. She struggled desperately as Morino pressed harder at her mouth. All she could see in her mind's eye now was May Sharp, on the bed, dead. Now there was pressure at her throat, tightening, tightening. There was Mannering smiling.

She felt a jolt at the back of her head, and lost consciousness.

.     .     .

"So you know where the ice is, do you?" Lanky Dan said to Mannering, as the girl fell. "If you want to live, you'll talk now." The words were bold, but his manner was nervous — as if Mannering's smile worried him.

"We got to get out of here," Morino muttered. "We just got to get out. There's the service lift, we can take 'em down in that. We'll shut *his* trap, then — "

As he spoke, he raised his cosh to attack Mannering — and, swift as light, Mannering dived for the door. Morino grabbed his arm. Mannering just smashed him back against the wall. He reached the door and opened it. Lanky Dan might not risk a shot, for fear of rousing others. That was Mannering's main hope.

Lanky Dan fired.

The roar of the shot and a fierce blow on Mannering's head came simultaneously. But he didn't lose consciousness. He opened the door and began to run. His mouth was open but he couldn't make a sound, it was like being in the grip of a nightmare.

He wanted to get help for the girl, help for himself, but his head was a black, screaming bag, and he couldn't think. He staggered as he ran, felt as if his head were splitting, was conscious only of the sense of movement.

On and on —

Back in the room, Morino clutched at Lanky Dan's gun arm, mouthing in terror:

"Get her out before the cops come, get her out!"


8

# SAD NIGHT FOR THE BARON

JOHN MANNERING came round, but did not have a high opinion of himself or of the pain in his head or the bright light. The voices of men and of one woman, which was very shrill, did more to distress him, and he almost wished that he had not come round. Not quite. He opened his eyes, and was not surprised to hear a man say:

"Look, he's waking up!"

A hush fell upon the crowd who had gathered about Mannering, and was welcome. He opened his eyes. He saw faces at curious angles; unshaven faces, shaven faces, and one smooth, powdered and painted face. This was cut into two by a red gash of a mouth, which was parted to show large white teeth; it was almost as if the woman were ready for a meal.

"Give him *air*," a man urged.

So someone had sense; there was always someone with sense.

Then another voice, deeper than any of these, came as if from a long way off, and a man said in a tone and with an emphasis which belonged at least as much to tradition as to the man himself:

"Now, then, what's going on here?"

This was the policeman.

Mannering opened his eyes again, and saw the tall helmet above a smooth, pale face; then the blue uniform and the glittering chromium of numbers on the collar, badge and other oddments.

The faces of the other people drew further away. Mannering knew now that he was lying on the ground, and that the people surrounded him. The brightness was from the sun, and there was a clear blue sky. His head ached as if he had been battered almost to death, his mouth was dry, his body ached.

The people talked.

"Who found him?"

"Jim did."

"Me."

"Lying just there, he was."

"Mind away, can't you, let him breathe." The constable was suddenly on his knees. "How do you feel, sir?"

Mannering moistened his lips.

"Dying," he said.

"Dy—" began the constable, startled.

"He's *dying*," breathed the woman, in what was nearly a subdued scream.

"Dying!"

"Now, stop that," rebuked the policeman sharply, "he's no more dying than I am." The man even looked sternly into Mannering's eyes, as if to say that he was in no condition to joke. "You'll be all right, sir. Let me just look at your head."

"He's bleeding," exclaimed the woman.

"Look here," said the policeman, testily, "if you can't stop shouting the odds, clear out of it."

59

"What, out of my own front garden?" She became shrilly indignant, angry. "I'll have you know—"

"Get me out of here," Mannering said in a weak voice, "and telephone the Yard. See if Bill—Superintendent—Bristow's there."

The policeman who had inspected the back of his head and knew that the wound, although messy, wasn't serious, looked hard at Mannering. Mannering's expression told him that his request was no joke.

"Bristow of the *Yard*," he asked.

"That's right."

"I—but I can't—say, who *are* you?" The policeman had grey eyes, rather pleasant ones, and they rounded and became very bright as the light of understanding dawned in them. He had seen this man before, and was beginning to realise where. "You're—Mr John Mannering."

"That's right."

"Here, Bert, hear that? This is *Man*nering. You know, that 'tec who . . ."

.       .       .

The stages of Mannering's journey to his flat, in Green Street, Chelsea, were several and varied, and all slow. First a doctor; next a Divisional Police Station with wary detectives; then Scotland Yard and Bill Bristow himself, a Scotland Yard stalwart who handled most of the stolen jewellery cases, and who was working on the Wannaker job.

Bristow talked to the police-surgeon.

"Obviously Mannering was suffering from concussion, it's a marvel he got as far as he did," the doctor said. "But you can do odd things with concussion."

Bristow forbore to say that he knew what concussion could do.

He talked to Mannering, realising that he learned no more of the story than Mannering wanted to tell him. . . .

In fact Mannering said he had not seen the two men's faces, because he thought that it was better not to give Bristow too good a chance to find and charge them — yet. For the rest, he told the truth.

Bristow knew that Mannering had run or walked over two miles before he had collapsed. Only a man with fantastic will power and great physical toughness could have done that; but he knew Mannering well enough not to be really surprised.

"All right, John," he said, "we'll get you home. Yes, we found May Sharp and we're looking for Helen Chadwick — we're looking for both the Chadwicks." He was heavy and almost grim. "I'll talk to you when your head's a bit easier."

"For all such mercies, humble thanks," said Mannering, whose head ached sullenly. "Let Lorna know, will you?"

"Yes," Bristow promised.

•    •    •

Being married to John Mannering made Lorna Mannering a woman to envy, in the eyes of many who knew Mannering only slightly. Others, who knew him better, were more inclined to sympathise with Lorna. Certainly there were burdens as well as ecstasy. At times Lorna was convinced that he should never have married; at others she believed him when he said that he couldn't live without her, life would be too drab and too dour.

The simple truth was that they were very like other married couples, with their ups and downs; perhaps the ups went higher and the downs fell lower than most.

When Lorna Mannering discovered that her husband

had not returned to the Green Street flat, which over-looked the distant Thames and the Embankment with its rows of plane trees, she was not surprised, for she knew he was on a case. Occasionally, cases worried and even alarmed her, but this one did not. She wasn't quite sure why. She knew little about it, except that a wealthy American had lost jewels, worth a fortune, which he had bought from Quinns. So her husband, owner of Quinns and being possessed of a conscience, was helping to get them back.

He had said little about it; nothing had suggested that violence might come into the affair.

In that half-guilty way which some creative artists have, Lorna was almost glad that she need not talk to him, think about what he was saying, and generally behave in wifely fashion. Ethel, the maid, was never bright in the morning, and that also suited Lorna perfectly. After a light breakfast, she climbed the loft-ladder which led from a passage to the studio above the flat and, once there, became a different woman.

She walked to the window and looked out. The sun was shining on the Thames, here and there were shimmering patches of the river's surface. A launch crowded with sightseers chugged cheerfully past. Traffic sped along the Embankment at a speed which suggested that traffic patrol police would soon be setting a trap and that the Public Exchequer would soon be benefiting from the fines thus earned.

She wasn't thinking about the police, but about the beauty of London as it sprawled, a spreading giant, beneath the June sun. It held her for a long time, and when she turned away she had a dreamy look. She put on a blue smock, which was liberally daubed with paint of a dozen colours, and then inspected a half-finished painting. She was renowned for her portraits, but this was different; this was the London scene that she saw every day from her studio window, put vividly on a great stretch of canvas.

John hadn't seen it yet; she was waiting eagerly for his opinion; the nearer it was to being finished when he did see it, the better.

Above all else, it was a labour of love.

She picked up her palette and knife, and began to work. She forgot everything but the contrast of subdued colour and the fascinating detail. Vaguely, she heard the telephone bell, the front door bell, the telephone bell again. Ethel wouldn't disturb her, no one would disturb her, because there was a gentleman's agreement that even her husband wouldn't interrupt her when she was working.

The telephone rang again, a tinkling noise, a long way off. That church – the sun touched the blue-grey slate spire with light which turned a strange colour, could she capture it? She mixed green and blue and red, dabbed – and there it was.

Her heart was light and her eyes glowed, she started again – and then a high-pitched voice sounded below the loft hatch, a loathsome interruption.

*"Excuse me, ma'am!"* Ethel had ambitions in opera and a voice which could be disconcerting. Now, she let it quaver, finding a good excuse for a little practice. "The telephone, ma'am! It's for you-*oo!*"

"Oh, damn," exclaimed Lorna, and more loudly: "All right, I'll take it."

There was a telephone in a corner, but the bell rang downstairs. Lorna did not think very much about the girl, was preoccupied with her colours and her angles, assumed that it was John, or –

"Hallo?"

"Mrs Mannering?" a man asked.

Perhaps it was because she had been married to Mannering for so long that she suddenly forgot the easel and the sunlit city. She did not like the voice, or the tone. There was an overlay of insolence in it: something she sensed more than understood.

"Yes."

"Mrs Mannering," the man said, "when Mannering comes home, tell him he'll get a much worse dose next time, he won't have any head left. And tell him that he'd better know where those sparklers are."

Lorna caught her breath. 'Much worse . . . no head left.' "Who —"

"Never mind who," the man said. "He'll know."

He rang off.

From that moment on until half-past twelve, when she had a message from Superintendent Bristow of the Yard, the morning was dark and bleak and there was no desire in her to paint the scene or capture the heart of London.

Bristow telephoned himself, was reassuring, but passed on the police-surgeon's advice to make Mannering rest for a few days.

"That's if you've any influence over him at all," Bristow said.

She didn't answer; no one could make Mannering rest if he felt the need for action.

·    ·    ·

A man helped Mannering up the stairs at Green Street, although that wasn't really necessary, Mannering could walk by himself. He looked pale, but his head wasn't bandaged; it wasn't until Lorna saw the back of his head that she noticed the piece of sticking plaster. He grinned at her. Ethel peered at him from the kitchen door and his guide, from the Yard, asked with great solicitude:

"All right now, sir?"

"Fine, Dawson, thanks very much."

"Pleasure, sir. Take it easy now."

"I always take it easy," Mannering said.

That set Detective Officer Dawson chuckling as he hurried down the stairs, but did not take the accusing look out of Lorna's eyes. For now that she was sure that Mannering was not badly hurt, she could tell him what she thought of him, and demand to know why he hadn't told her that it was this kind of case. She had a constant theme: "I must *know*, darling."

"Sorry, sweet," he said, grinning in a way which was intended to melt her mood. "I didn't think Dizzy would come into the open. Just a little miscalculation."

"I know that kind of miscalculation," said Lorna coldly.

"Have a heart," pleaded Mannering. "Here am I, battered about the head, at death's door for at least twenty minutes, and what do I get? I get — "

"What you deserve," Lorna said tartly. "You'd better come into the study and sit down." She led the way, and was punching a cushion into the right position in a chair when he slid his arms round her waist and almost squeezed the breath out of her.

"Fool!"

"See how ill I am," said Mannering, earnestly.

"Idiot!"

"Yes, dear," said Mannering, and his eyes quizzed her; and she stood looking into them for a few seconds. It seemed a long time. They told her a story which nothing else would. Her mood changed. She didn't smile, but she relaxed, went to the kitchen and told Ethel to make coffee, very hot, and then came back. By then, Mannering was smoking.

"Is it very bad?" she asked. "I mean, the case."

"Not good, my sweet."

"Why?"

"May Sharp was murdered." He paused. "Remember May? The girl with the fair hair who works for Stocker, and — "

65

Lorna said slowly: "Yes, I remember her."

"I can't quite make it out," Mannering said. "Whether it was in mistake for someone else, or whether it was because of something she discovered, we can't say yet."

"Does Bristow know?"

"Part of it. He's coming here soon for the inside story." A brighter gleam showed in Mannering's eyes. "Our William's in a sunny mood, and taking me on trust. What fools men are! In fact, I think the Yard's had a tip from the Home Office who have had a courteous request for gentleness from the United States Embassy. Saul Wannaker is quite an industrial giant –he's over here on some big deal – you ought to paint him, honeybunch, he's a typical Yankee. Even to the beard." Not all of the flippancy was forced. "But I like him. So will you."

"Is he coming, too?"

"Yes. Also Jeff Wannaker, who travels the world in his father's interests – a kind of super-salesman it seems. You've met and approved of Jeff, haven't you?"

"I haven't any anti-American bias," Lorna said.

Coffee came in, hot and very strong. Ethel managed to snatch a glance at Mannering's head, and clicked her tongue impulsively in distress and sympathy. When she went out, closing the door with a snap, Lorna said in a tone which meant business:

"Just what did happen?"

He told her the whole story. His word picture of Helen Chadwick really made her feel anxious; she could almost see the American girl, almost hear her voice when she had telephoned.

"So I went to see her," Mannering said. "She sounded as if she were in the presence of death." He lit a cigarette before going on very quietly: "And I was completely foxed, my sweet. I thought that they'd

66

killed May Sharp in mistake for Helen – using someone who didn't know Helen by sight. They wouldn't expect a stand-in. I didn't dream that they were still on the scene. I didn't even look in the wardrobe, although the door was ajar." He was quietly angry with himself; and bitter, too. "Now they've a pair of prisoners – both Chadwicks. If they never show up again, blame me."

"But, darling, the police – "

"Oh, they'll look for the Chadwicks and for the mob, but let's face probabilities. Robbie Chadwick might be in hiding because he stole the jewels from Wannaker, and Helen might have joined him in hiding because she killed May Sharp. The police can't be sure when May was killed. Even my story doesn't clear her. Look at the motive that's staring the Yard in the face – that May found out that Helen knew where the jewels were. It shouts along Whitehall, along Parliament Street and right into Bristow's window. Obviously Helen could have killed May Sharp, and keeping her quiet could be the motive. I don't think she did, but it could have happened. Bristow has to work on evidence even if it's circumstantial."

"So the hunt's on for Helen Chadwick," Lorna said.

"All London and the Home Counties police have been alerted and a general call's going out – it's probably gone by now. But let's see it Ben's way."

"This Ben," Lorna said slowly, "what's his voice like?"

Mannering looked at her with the smile which was on the lips of the painted Cavalier.

"Deep, with an echo of a sneer in it. The voice of a man used to getting his own way. The pedantic might say cultured. It's an educated voice – rather as if something out of the jungle has been given a veneer of education. Has he telephoned?"

67

"Yes."

"Offer?"

"Just that you've got to hand over the jewels. Why does he think you have the jewels?"

"Oh, I told them that I had," said Mannering. "I wanted a breathing space, and that gave me one. I hoped to get out and slam the door and cry blue murder, to bring help for Helen. Instead I blacked out, and apparently went off by the back door – unseen. The others also got away before anyone came, only an old woman heard the shots, and she telephoned the night porter."

He paused, before adding gruffly: "I just ran until I collapsed. But when I came round, I remembered everything clearly enough." He paused again, then went on bitterly: "Poor Helen. She thought she was out of the wood."

Lorna didn't speak. She had a figure to which the years had been kind, and her beauty was dark and at times almost brooding. In moments like this, she could look sullen.

She made herself say: "How much does Bristow know?"

"Everything but the names of Morino and Lanky Dan. He knows there's a Ben," said Mannering. "When the mob knows the police haven't got the names of the trio they may hope I'll do a deal with them. And who knows what might happen next? There's the reputation of the Chadwicks, danger to Helen, the loss of the jewels, and – "

"Go on, finish it," Lorna said. "What else?"

Mannering said quietly: "Wannaker, the old boy, was also robbed of some highly confidential trade figures, including details of a big dollar deal which will send certain British industrial stocks sky-high. If anyone has foreknowledge, they can make a fortune. The question is – do the thieves know the value of the

68

papers? Dizzy's in this, and it's the kind of job he'd revel in. But the others — ''

Mannering broke off, and shrugged.

Before he could go on there was a sharp ring at the front-door bell.

Ethel walked across the hall and opened the door. A moment later, a woman's voice came, clear, high-pitched, obviously American, as obviously alarmed.

"Is Mr Mannering here, please? I must see him, will you tell him that? Just tell him it's Mrs Saul Wannaker, and I'm in a great hurry.''

## 9

## ELAINE

MANNERING moved towards the door, and saw Elaine Wannaker coming in, looking as if she could hardly restrain herself from pushing past Ethel. At sight of him, her beautiful blue eyes rounded, her long eye-lashes seemed to quiver, and she ran towards him with arms outstretched. She clutched his hands, and almost jumped into his arms.

"Oh, John," she cried. "John!"

Lorna stood in the doorway, calm with a touch of aloofness. Ethel gaped. Elaine Wannaker put her soft cheek against Mannering's shoulder, and held him tightly, as if she felt that this was her last link with hope.

"I just can't tell you how glad I am to see you," she cried. "I just can't tell you, it's been *terrible*."

Mannering tried to unlink hands.

"Just terrible," repeated Elaine Wannaker, and opened her eyes. As she was leaning on Mannering's right shoulder, she looked straight at Lorna, who had not moved from the doorway. "Oh my dear!" she gasped, and moved back. Powder was left on Mannering's coat and there was a smear of lipstick on his cheek. "Oh, I didn't know you had *com*pany," she breathed.

"Too bad," said Mannering breathlessly. "And hardly company. Darling, this is Mrs Elaine Wannaker, Elaine, this is my wife."

The moment of silence would have been heavy but for the gleam which sprang into Lorna's eyes, and took the shadow of strain out of Mannering's. Then it was Elaine who triumphed over the circumstances of her own making. She turned and rushed towards Lorna with arms outstretched, showing just as much enthusiasm. Lorna found her arms going out, allowed her hands to be gripped tightly.

"Why, it's good to know you, Mrs Mannering! I just couldn't wait until John let me meet you. Aren't you *proud* of John? If I were his wife, I'd be so proud I wouldn't know how to look at another man."

"I'm sure you wouldn't," Lorna said weakly.

"I just wouldn't look at another man," Elaine insisted, "and that's as true as I'm here. But don't misunderstand me, Mrs Mannering, I'm a *very* happily married woman, John will vouch for that — won't you, John?"

"Most certainly I will," said Mannering dryly.

Lorna's eyes glistened, but she watched the American woman closely. Elaine Wannaker was something to be admired. Small, almost tiny, she had a dream-like figure, and was superbly dressed. It was almost as if a piece of Dresden china had become animated. Her movements had grace and yet might almost have been due to a puppet master of supreme skill pulling the strings. Her face was pink with delight — the face of all the chocolate-box beauties and all the front row chorus girls of the century. She was like a lovely blossom, living her brief week of beauty until the frost of middle age withered her. Her make-up was perfect, it was easy to believe that her eyes were as naturally radiant, almost luminous, as they seemed to be. But they were not like Helen Chadwick's, even then. Her hair was auburn, beautifully massed in curls beneath an absurd little yellow hat, which was the last word in the world's little hats. She wore a dress of some shimmering green material, and it fitted her like a sheath – the kind of dream-dress that would bring wolf whistles from the coarse or the unkind, and whispers from women who could not wear one like it if they tried throughout their lives. Her gloves, shoes and bag were yellow.

Everything about her was chic; *petite*; and looked so expensive that it was hard to believe it was all real. The diamonds on her fingers and at her ears, the perfume, the jewelled clasp of her handbag.

"And I'm so worried about Saul," Elaine Wannaker declared. "I really am so worried, John, I don't know what to do."

"What's worrying about Saul?" asked Mannering.

It was only now that he was beginning to remember that he had a nasty wound on the back of his head, had been drugged and knocked about and given little time to rest. His head began to ache – not only at the back but across the front. There was a throbbing pain between his eyes. His skin felt tight. He wanted to sit down, but made himself stand there watching Wannaker's wife – and incidentally Jeff Wannaker's step-mother. Usually she amused him, and she ought to amuse him now; instead, he felt irritated. If Lorna had been affronted, he would have been angry; as it was, Lorna saved the day.

"Oh, John, I wouldn't worry you without a reason," Elaine declared, and her eyes gleamed as she rolled them. "He's gone away."

"But I was talking to him on the telephone not much more than an hour ago!"

"Yes, I know, he said he was coming to see you, and then he had another telephone call and he ran out on me. He did, he was actually *angry* when I asked him where he was going and why he looked so pale."

Mannering didn't speak. Lorna glanced at him swiftly, understanding the new alarm which showed in his eyes.

"Did he say what was worrying him?"

"No he wouldn't say," Elaine declared, "but it was frightening, John, really it was. He went to the telephone, why I *called* him. I could see him coming. He smiled at me the way he usually does and called me honey, and then – well, I handed him the telephone. He just talked it, and said 'yep', you know, the way he does, and the very next minute he looked *awful*."

Mannering said slowly, carefully: "He just spoke to someone on the telephone, and it shocked him. Is that it?"

"I should just say it did shock him! Why, he went so pale you wouldn't believe a man could change like it in just one second. And his eyes, they were *horrified* – that's the only word. He just banged down the receiver, and stood there looking at me, and do you know I don't think he *saw* me."

That must have been the insult beyond all her understanding.

"And what then?" Mannering asked. With new facts hammering at him his head ached more, and he sat slowly on the arm of a chair. He needed to make his own pace, not to be forced to hers.

"Why, I said to him, 'Saul, why are you looking like that, what's the matter?' And all he did was to turn away and go to the door, as sure as I'm standing here. I ran after him and asked him where he was going, and

72

he shook me *off*." Her voice rose. "He was so mad that he actually shook me off."

That was easy to imagine. She was lovely as a butterfly was lovely, she fluttered, she would show a foolish, affected concern, and if the news Wannaker had received had really hurt him, he would want to thrust her away. And he had.

"And he went out, I saw him get into a taxi," Elaine said, "one was passing along the street just when he reached it. Saul has the damnedest luck sometimes."

"A taxi," Mannering said. "A new one? Old one?"

"Well, it was just one of those boxes you call cabs in this city," Elaine said scathingly, "I wouldn't know whether it was new or old, they all look the same to me."

"Was Saul alone?"

"Why surely."

"What made you come rushing to me?"

"I just had to see *some*one," Elaine declared, "and I couldn't think of anyone else. I suppose I could have told Jeff but you know how it is between me and Jeff."

"I know how it is," Mannering agreed, and sounded gruff. "I still don't understand why you thought it worth while coming to me. Saul had a telephone call and it scared him. You could have called me about that."

"But—but you asked me to tell you of anything unusual that happened," Elaine said, and dropped her eyes as well as her voice. "Besides, I'm worried about Saul, I really am. I can't imagine what's got into him. If you'd seen the look he gave me, you would know what I mean. John, you don't know of any reason why Saul should treat me like that, do you?"

Her eyes were very wide open; so round and bright.

"I don't know of any reason at all," Mannering said. "Is there anything else?"

"Why, I guess not."

"This man who telephoned—did he give a name?"

"No, he didn't give any name at all," Elaine said slowly. "And I tell you, John, I didn't like the man the moment I heard his voice, it wasn't a voice *I'd* like to have—it was *cruel*, if you know what I mean. Kind of—" she waved her hands helplessly, as if trying to find the right word. "Well, it kind of scared me."

"I know that kind of voice," Mannering said, and moved towards the telephone. His head was splitting as he dialled Whitehall 1212, while Elaine stared at him, as if begging him to tell her what he was doing.

Scotland Yard answered.

"Is Superintendent Bristow there?" Mannering asked, and after a pause, went on: "Yes, I'll hold on." He looked up at Elaine, who fluttered more than ever, and who came running towards him.

"No, John, don't," breathed Elaine, "don't tell the police, I mean." She hissed the words, as if hoping that she wouldn't be heard on the telephone. "I just picked up an extension. The man said that if Saul helped the police, then—"

Bristow spoke into Mannering's ear.

"Who's the woman who doesn't want police co-operation?" he asked dryly.

"Hold on, please," Mannering said, as if casually, and pressed the receiver against his hand, tightly. "What's that, Elaine?"

"Oh, I should have told you! Just before he rang off the man was most emphatic, Saul wasn't to help the police at *all*. That was the only thing I heard."

Mannering seemed to hesitate, then put the telephone to his mouth and went on briskly: "I'm sorry, I don't want to speak to Superintendent Bristow after all." He rang off on Bristow's explosive comment, then stood up slowly; the pain at his head grew worse. "Elaine, why don't you learn how to tell a story?"

74

"I'm sorry, but I didn't know you were going to telephone that man Bristow, did I?"

"Did Saul say anything about telling the police?"

"He just walked out on me, the way I've told you."

"I see," said Mannering, and stood up; and swayed. Lorna hurried forward. Mannering went pale and dropped back into the chair. Elaine saw the adhesive plaster at the back of his head, as well as the broken skin and bruises at the temple.

She put her hands to her lips as if to stifle a scream.

"Sorry," Mannering said, and closed his eyes. "I'll be all right. Better go into — the bedroom," he added, and forced a smile at Elaine. Lorna helped him up and into the bedroom, yet he had strength to close the door. He grinned at her. "Darling," he said, "you've a job on your hands."

Lorna stood away, sharply.

"I wasn't fooling all the time," Mannering said, and caught her hand. "Look after Elaine. Go where she goes, talk to her, try to find out whether she's hiding anything, will you? She might well be. And get her out of here before Bristow comes. I want to talk to him alone, and Elaine doesn't like him."

"What's more to the point is whether he likes her," Lorna said.

"Oh, come! She's well-meaning, I should say, and her Saul dotes on her. I'd like to know what Ben said to him to make him brush her off. She didn't like it, did she?"

"She wouldn't like any man who refused to let her tread on him," Lorna said coldly. "Obviously she is very attached to you."

"That's just the build-up that Saul gave me, he had to win her over before he could really get moving on the case!" Mannering grinned. "Be good, my sweet, be helpful."

"I'll do what I can," Lorna promised grudgingly,

75

"but I don't guarantee that I won't strangle her. What excuse shall I make for leaving the flat?"

Mannering considered; and then slowly smiled, and raised his eyes upwards, but not in invocation; more as if he had been inspired.

"Why not show her the studio and make tea up there? She'll almost certainly want her portrait painted after that. It will be a nice fat commission in dollars, we could go over and spend the spoils next year."

Lorna drew further back.

"There are times when I could actively dislike you," she said coldly. "I hope your headache gets worse."

She went out.

Two minutes later, she was back.

"The special tablets are in the top drawer, I shifted them," she said. "I'd take two if I were you, one won't help you much. You look dreadful."

Mannering managed to blow her a kiss. She went out again. He sat with his eyes closed. The sound of voices outside gradually faded, and he thought he heard the two women going up the loft-ladder. Then silence fell, a blessed quiet; he hoped that it would go on a long time.

It was broken by a ring at the front-door bell. This would be Bristow.

It was Saul Wannaker.

10

## WANNAKER

MANNERING was still in the bedroom when Saul Wannaker went across to his study. Ethel shut him in,

then tiptoed to the bedroom door and tapped lightly.
Mannering called:

"It's all right."

He looked at himself in the mirror. His eyes were
bloodshot, and his pallor was alarming, but he didn't
look at death's door. The worst thing about all this
was that he needed to be at his best: Wannaker's own
behaviour was puzzling, and he ought to be trapped
into admitting why he had hurried out of the Park Lane
apartment where he and his wife were staying.

Mannering straightened his tie, smoothed down his
hair, had a sip of water, and then went to the study.
This was a small room, with a desk set slantwise in a
corner so that the window light fell straight on to it;
and with Regency furniture which had a pleasant
homeliness. It was his favourite room, and where he
and Lorna spent their time when they were on their
own.

Saul Wannaker stood up, slowly. Had Mannering
not been forewarned, he would have noticed nothing
unusual about the man. As it was, the signs of strain
at the eyes and mouth were unmistakable. But Wannaker smiled. He often smiled — but this was the first
time Mannering had known him to do so as if to hide
signs of strain.

"Hi, John," he said, and then looked concerned.
"Say, they really have been laying into you. Doesn't
your head hurt?"

"It could be worse," Mannering said brightly. "How
are things with you?"

"Oh, fine," said Wannaker. "That is, as fine as
they can be with a man who still doesn't know whether
he's rich or poor. The jewels hardly matter, but if that
other thing leaks out — " he shrugged. "It will cause
a panic on Wall Street and the Stock Exchange over
here. I'm hoping that you've discovered something,
and that's why you've sent for me."

There wasn't a word about the telephone call; the threats; his behaviour with his wife; but the tell-tale signs at his eyes and mouth talked of them.

"I've discovered something," Mannering said, "and it isn't good. Bristow will be here in a few minutes, I'll tell you both at the same time." He proffered cigarettes. "Where's Jeff?"

"He's fine," declared Wannaker, "just fine." He smiled as he drew on the cigarette, said nothing about having been warned off the police. "Well, I guess that's one way of putting it. He's having himself a new experience, John."

"What's new for him?"

"Well, you may not believe it, but he's never been in love," said Wannaker. "He hasn't had all that time for women, I guess, but that sister of Robbie Chadwick certainly did something to him. He hasn't talked about much else since he saw her last night. I wonder if you'll let me see her before Jeff talks to her again, John, I'd like to see what kind of girl she is. Maybe a word in the right place now would save him a lot of trouble later on."

"I wish I could promise that you'll see her first," Mannering began. "That's why — "

The door bell rang again. This time, it was Bristow. Wannaker didn't turn a hair.

. . .

As Mannering talked, he watched the two men closely. Their reaction to the story was very different, as markedly as one would expect from two most dissimilar men. Bristow was tall, lean, well-knit and brisk-moving, giving an impression of confidence and ability. He wasn't particularly handsome, in spite of good features. He was pale, and his eyes were grey and rather dull, at times; they could spark with emotion,

78

and emotion made him much better-looking. He was dressed in light grey, and wore a wilting gardenia in his lapel. His manner was brisk to a point of sharpness.

Saul Wannaker was two inches shorter, but still on the high side of medium height. In his early fifties, he might have looked in the forties but for his sparse grey hair and large bald patch. His face had a weathered look like the face of a sailor; he did a great deal of sailing in Long Island Sound. It was round, and his eyes were bright brown, his nose was rounded, his features chubby, his little beard fluffy. He was a comfortable man to look at and to talk to; few would have dreamed that he was Big Business, and in control of millions of dollars. Some said billions. He wore rimless glasses, and was inclined to blink a lot. Even now, with the anxiety that he hadn't talked about on his mind, he had a comforting kind of look. People would feel safe with him.

Mannering told the story —

". . . And that's as far as I've gone," he finished, leaning back and lighting a cigarette. The effort of talking hadn't helped, but Lorna's tablets had; he didn't feel half as bad as he expected. "That's the plain, unvarnished truth, Bill."

Bristow wasn't smiling.

"So you told them you had the diamonds," he said heavily.

"Yes."

"If I may say so," Wannaker interrupted, "that was a very courageous thing to do, John. It isn't many people who would turn the attention of criminals of this kind on to themselves, just to save someone else."

Mannering murmured: "Nice of you. But look how much Helen has to thank me for."

"Listen," said Bristow, "with a head like yours,

you ought to have lain down and died — don't start blaming yourselves because Helen Chadwick's missing. You say these men seem certain that Chadwick stole the jewels."

"We're finding that out, aren't we?" Mannering murmured.

"See here," said Wannaker abruptly, "I don't like the way this affair is shaping. I'd like to get those jewels back, and know about those market arrangements but not at the price of people's lives. No, sir. This dead girl, what was her name?"

"May Sharp," Mannering said.

"Where did she come into it?"

Mannering said slowly: "She was just trying to help. It was her job."

Wannaker said abruptly, almost violently: "I don't want to risk any more lives, gentlemen, and that's my last word on it. I'd like to get the affair settled, but the loss doesn't hurt me or my wife that bad. There's no sign yet that the market's being played, and I guess I'll take my chance on that. From this moment on, you can count me out of this. I'm through."

He stood up.

Bristow said slowly, thoughtfully: "We have the jewels to find, Mr Wannaker, and we have a murderer to find. We go on, whatever you do. And if there's any way in which you can help us, then your duty — "

"Superintendent," said Wannaker, making the title sound pompous, even a little ridiculous, "I don't have to be told my duty, thank you. The police must do what they think fit, but I don't have to stay in the hunt. I hired Mr Mannering, in a way of speaking, to find the jewels, and he employed this poor woman whose throat was cut. She died because she was being paid in my money — isn't that right, John?"

"It's a way to look at it."

"Well, from this moment on, I'm out of all this,"

80

said Wannaker. "I'm right out. It will take me a long time to get this off my conscience."

He stood up.

Bristow seemed bereft of words. Mannering murmured a platitude. Wannaker, in his comforting, half-smiling way, picked up his hat and followed Mannering to the door. Mannering closed it on him, then stepped swiftly into the drawing room and looked down into Green Street.

Bristow joined him.

Wannaker had a taxi waiting. It moved off as soon as he climbed in, and Mannering took a pencil out of his pocket and scribbled on his shirt cuff; K12EGM.

"K12EGM," he said aloud. "Make a note of that, Bill, we might find it useful if we want to know where he's been."

Bristow asked heavily: "What got into him?"

"He's got a death on his conscience," Mannering said heavily. "Or something on his mind. His wife was telling me about it. I should say that the man we know as Ben has started threatening Wannaker – saying, 'stop employing Mannering, or else'. That kind of thing. It might be a simple threat to murder his butterfly beauty," Mannering went on. "Bill, I don't like any of this."

Bristow said: "That girl Sharp liked it less. I know what you think but I'm not sure you're right. Helen Chadwick may have killed May Sharp. You don't know that she didn't. For all you know, the other men were in her room simply to make it seem more plausible that she was being attacked. These Chadwicks may have fooled you. I've known you make a fool of yourself over a pair of pretty eyes before."

Mannering didn't speak.

"What are you going to do next?" Bristow demanded.

"The same as you," Mannering said meekly. "Look

81

for Helen and Robbie Chadwick, and try to find out why Wannaker was so shaken this afternoon." He told Bristow what had happened at Wannaker's apartment, and why he had telephoned the Yard, then went on softly: "He has an Achilles heel, and we want to find it."

"*I* want the Chadwicks," Bristow growled.

"And the gang who've been menacing Helen," murmured Mannering. "This Ben and his boys."

Bristow said heavily: "John, sometimes you're clever and you always have plenty of nerve. But you aren't always right. You think Helen Chadwick's on the level, but where's the evidence? Just in her eyes?" That was nearly a sneer. "See it this way. Her brother stole the jewels. She came to England to help get him out of the mess. He had to hide. Ben and these men were working with her brother, and she knew it. But she had to try to smash the case against her brother, so she worked out this plot story. She pretends to be threatened by her actual accomplices. They go through the motions of menacing her, but in fact that's all to convince you that she's in real trouble – to convince you that a third party's involved."

Mannering was able to grin, in spite of his aching head.

"What's funny?" demanded Bristow tartly.

"Just my silly thoughts," apologised Mannering. "Don't go into more detail, Bill. You think that this business with Ben and his boys might be a front to help the Chadwicks get away with the jewels. Right?"

"It could be."

"Not on your life," Mannering declared, "and you know it. I'll tell you someone who will tell you where to get off if you start throwing doubt on the virtue of Helen Chadwick."

"Who?"

"Jeff, son of Saul Wannaker."

"I'm getting tired of this family," Bristow growled. "I never like jobs with Americans involved, they don't think the same way as we do. Anyhow, what do I care if Jeff Wannaker approves of me? *I* think that the Chadwicks are taking you for a ride," Bristow went on vigorously. "Unless you're taking us all for a ride." He brooded, eyeing Mannering morosely. "You haven't got the Wannaker jewels, have you?"

"No, sir," said Mannering.

"I can never be sure with you," Bristow muttered. "You get worse as you grow older, sometimes I think I preferred it when you were the Baron. I did know where I stood with a thief. This way, I'm never really sure I know what side you're on."

Mannering smiled sweetly, "I never was the Baron, Bill, and never a thief. You know I'm on May Sharp's side, don't you?"

Bristow grunted.

.    .    .

When the Yard man had gone, Mannering sat back, to keep his aching head quite still. He could think rationally, but another black-out would do a lot of harm.

So could Bristow—

Was Bristow right?

.    .    .

Whatever else, Elaine Wannaker's troubled spirit had been soothed by the hour or two in the studio.

Lorna had expected to hear squeaks and squeals of affected delight; and instead had been met with a shrewd appreciation of the canvases. Lorna had almost enjoyed herself, and but for the knowledge of what had happened and what would probably happen next, she would have withdrawn the 'almost'. She mellowed considerably towards Wannaker's wife, and told Mannering so when they went downstairs after tea.

"Lorna, dear, I do wish you'd come and see the pictures Saul has bought me in London," Elaine said earnestly. "I think they're just wonderful, but I would simply love your opinion. That's if John could spare you for an hour or two?" She was arch.

"Of course, Elaine," said Mannering. "When?"

"There's no time like the present, is there?" Elaine spoke as if she were making a remark both profound and original. "*Can* you come right now, Lorna?"

Lorna hesitated; and was lost.

Mannering saw them to the street, feeling better than he had, but promising Lorna that he would take it easy. Lorna led the way to their lock-up garage, nearby, and took out the cream-coloured Rolls-Bentley which made the Mannerings the envy of all the small children and most auto enthusiasts in the district.

She pulled up outside the apartment block in Park Lane, twenty minutes later. A commissionaire saluted as they got out. The entrance was in a side street; one of elegance and unostentatious luxury. There was no single flat in the building cheaper than thirty pounds a week.

Elaine was chatting; about paintings, etchings, books, all in a genuinely knowledgeable way. She now led the way to the second-floor flat, and was opening her bag for the key when a man leapt at her from an alcove five yards away.

A knife glinted in his hand.

# 11

# ATTACK

ELAINE WANNAKER screamed.

Lorna saw the steel glint, felt her heart bound, but couldn't move or utter a sound. It looked as if the knife would bury itself in Elaine's breast as she stood with her mouth wipe open and the scream shivering out. The man was small, little more than a boy, with a lot of black hair – and with most of his face covered by a black scarf.

Elaine flung herself to one side.

The movement seemed to release Lorna from the paralysis. The assailant was off his balance, and she kicked and struck at him at the same time. She caught him a glancing blow, more by luck than judgment; because he was unsteady, he sprawled against the wall. The blade of the knife stuck into the wall.

Elaine's scream rose and fell, like a wailing siren. She crouched against the wall, watching the man, seeing him steady, straighten up, and snatch at the knife again. Then the door of the apartment opened and Saul Wannaker appeared.

The youth saw him.

He turned and ran towards the landing, the lift and the head of the stairs. Wannaker jumped after him, but Elaine moved again, stifling the scream, and flung herself into Wannaker's arms. He simply had to hold her. The youth reached the corner and disappeared. Lorna, her heart steadying, turned desperately to follow, but Wannaker called:

"Ma'am, you stay right here!"

Elaine was sobbing now, and clutching at Wannaker; Lorna could see that she was shivering. Wannaker smoothed down her hair, awkwardly; as if he did not want to do it, and the display of emotion embarrassed him.

The assailant's footsteps faded.

"We haven't done a thing to catch him," Lorna said angrily. "We must! You telephone, I'll go." She turned and ran, ignoring Wannaker's repeated calls. At the landing, she hesitated; had the man taken the lift or the stairs? Could she hope to catch up with him? She didn't wait for the lift but ran down the stairs. The commissionaires might be in time to stop the little beast, he couldn't have gone far across that spacious hall.

She jumped two stairs, turned a corner and almost cannoned into a tall, youthful-looking man, who was already looking puzzled.

"Why, Mrs Mannering, what's all this?" It was Jeff Wannaker.

"Did you see," Lorna began, and discovered that she was breathless. "Did you see — a man — running?"

The stuttering beat of a motor-cycle engine came clearly above her voice. She felt sure that it was the assailant. But now that she had stopped running it was difficult to start again, and Jeff was gripping her arm.

"Say, what is all this?"

"He tried to kill — your mother. Elaine. He — "

"Jumping catfish!" Jeff roared, and let her go and ran towards the front door. The sunlit street was deserted when he reached it, except for a nursemaid coming along, pushing a pram. The staccato note of the motor-cycle engine faded into silence.

Lorna joined him.

A commissionaire, who had been out of sight, came hurrying, letting a door slam behind him.

"Is anything wrong?" He was alarmed.

"Gone, by heck," Jeff said, and looked ruefully into Lorna's face. "I was that much too late. Didn't even get a look at the motor-cycle." He turned to the commissionaire. "Did you see a man come in just now, and ride off on a motor-cycle?"

"I heard it all right. And I saw him come in, too — a little chap. What's wrong? What'll we do?"

The lift doors opened and Saul Wannaker appeared, striding forward.

"Jeff," he called. There was command in his face, and his bland, rubicund face held an expression that would have surprised everyone except those who knew him at a board meeting when affairs were going wrong. "We won't do a thing until we've discussed it." He looked at Lorna, and behind his glasses his eyes were cold, inquisitive. He didn't actually say "who is this?" but his expression asked the question.

"Sure, Dad," Jeff said, and forced a smile. "Say, you two don't know each other, do you? Dad, this is Mrs Mannering. Lorna, this is my father."

"Mrs Mannering!" Wannaker's expression changed, he smiled broadly and came forward quickly, heartily. "Why, I'd no idea! Let's go upstairs, Elaine isn't so good."

"Hurt?" Jeff asked sharply.

Lorna looked at him thoughtfully. Something in his voice suggested that he didn't waste much affection on his step-mother. It was almost as if he hoped that she had been hurt.

"No, just scared." His father appeared to notice nothing unusual. "Mrs Mannering, I can't say what a pleasure it is to know you, and how grateful I am for . . ."

He went on talking.

The commissionaire watched them get into the lift, closed the outer doors, and then scratched his chin. Two or three other people came out of the warmth of the street into this cool arbour of luxury.

Lorna was in one corner, the two Wannakers were close together. She sensed the tension between them;

perhaps nothing stronger than the restraint born of anxiety. Jeff looked — hard; purposeful. So did his father. It came to her mind that the Wannakers seemed scared.

The apartment door was closed.

Wannaker opened it with a key, and they stood aside for Lorna to go in. The small hall, with its gilt mirrors and futuristic paintings, was empty, but several doors stood open, and Lorna saw Elaine sitting back in a huge red chair. Approaching her with a small bottle in her hand was a coal-black negress dressed in black and white, with a round, anxious face and yet a look of confidence.

"Ma'am, yo' just take a deep smell of this, yo'll feel fine as soon as yo've done that. Now, ma'am!" She spoke as she might to a child.

Elaine sat up, and sniffed, delicately; sniffed again; then looked at Lorna and the men. Her expression changed. Lorna had a feeling which she talked about to Mannering later that evening: a conviction that Elaine Wannaker was a competent little actress. Everything she did bore that out; her entrance at the flat, her trick of flinging herself bodily at anyone around, were all part of an act: or they might be.

"It's all right, Mary, I'll look after Mrs Wannaker," Saul declared. "You get on with whatever you were doing."

"Yes, sah." The maid gave a nervous smile. "Yo' just make her smell them crystals, sah, she'll feel real fine after that. Maybe some hot coffee, too —"

"Sure, that's an idea, some hot coffee," Jeff agreed.

"Right away, sah, right away." The maid hurried off.

Saul Wannaker sat on the arm of his wife's chair, and held her hand.

"Are you feeling better, honey?"

"I'll be all right, I guess," Elaine said tearfully. "I
88

was so scared I don't know what I would have done if Lorna hadn't been right with me." She smiled at Lorna with forced brightness. If she had felt as badly as she had made out, would she have been able to act like this now?

Jeff was looking down at her, with an expression of disdain. Disdain — or dislike? All of this was worth talking to John about.

"I did nothing," Lorna said, "you were so quick."

"Why, I just felt as if I couldn't move to save my life when I saw that knife coming right at me — " Elaine broke off, closed her eyes, and looked as if she were about to have the vapours.

She didn't.

The Wannakers listened to the story, and neither of them showed any desire to telephone the police. It wasn't Lorna's responsibility, but she felt uneasy. There was something odd about this family; it might be because of the domestic tensions, or it might be because of fear. Fear could turn beautiful things ugly.

Mary brought in coffee on a silver tray.

"Why, that's just what I wanted, Mary, thank you," Elaine said, very sweetly, and smiled brightly as the maid went out. "Saul, I feel so bad about all this, I'd asked Lorna to come and look at those pictures you bought yesterday. We just have to show them to her. Why she's a genius, I spent a wonderful afternoon looking at her paintings. You'd never believe how good they are. Say, Saul honey, before I leave London I want my portrait painted by Lorna Mannering, R.A. *And* nothing *you* say is going to stop me from getting it, I'm only worried in case Lorna hasn't any time."

Lorna didn't speak.

Wannaker said: "I'm sure that Mrs Mannering would make time for you, honey."

"Yes," Lorna was surprised that her voice was so

sharp. "Yes, of course. But aren't you going to find time to call the police?"

No one spoke.

Jeff grinned, and turned away. He thrust his hands deep into his pockets, and Lorna had an odd impression; that he was whistling under his breath. There was a long pause and then Elaine echoed: *"Police"*, as if she had been momentarily bewildered, and was only now able to assume her part again.

"No, ma'am," Saul Wannaker said firmly, "we are not going to call the police. I don't mind telling you that I wish I'd never reported the theft of those diamonds to the authorities, it's caused so much trouble, and already there's one woman's life on my conscience. From now on I'm not going to do a thing, ma'am."

Lorna didn't speak.

"Don't you think that will look pretty queer?" asked Jeff, turning round from the mirror in which he had been straightening his tie.

"I don't care what it looks like," Wannaker said. "I'm going to try to finish my business in this country quickly, and then go home. I don't like it here any more."

"You're making Mrs Mannering—" began Jeff.

"I don't mean any offence to Mrs Mannering," Wannaker said. He looked not only self-possessed but in complete control of the situation: and his voice suggested that he was explaining to a small boy out of the kindness of his heart, not because he thought that it would do the slightest good. "I've already told John that I'm withdrawing from this case. I didn't tell him the real reason why. Perhaps you'll tell him for me," he added, and brought his gaze to bear on Lorna. Behind those lenses, they were fine, grey eyes; and steady and direct.

"If you'll tell me," Lorna said.

"I'm about to, Mrs Mannering. I won't have anything more to do with the police or with your husband or with anyone connected with this case, because a few hours ago I had a telephone call threatening my wife with violence if I didn't withdraw. I went to see the man who telephoned me and talked to him. I believe he meant what he said. You've seen some of the evidence, ma'am. So, I won't lift a finger. If it were myself I would go on with it, but when my wife's life is at stake – ''

He broke off.

Elaine was looking at him as if at a hero. Her eyes were wet.

Jeff said gruffly: ''You please yourself, I'm going to help all I can.''

''Jeff, do me a favour, will you?'' his father asked mildly. ''Don't come to any decision until you've had time to think about it. That man with the knife was serious.''

''I've had plenty of time to think,'' Jeff growled. ''You've let a guy scare you. That doesn't mean that I have to be scared too. He hasn't threatened me.''

His father's lips set tightly.

''Jeff, honey, I don't understand you,'' Elaine broke in, in a subdued voice. ''I'd be glad to take any risks if I thought it would help, but how will it help, can you tell me that?'' Her eyes were starry and questing and so innocent. ''What could Saul do if he was willing to take risks with *me*?''

Jeff said abruptly: ''The hoodlum who's threatened you thinks Dad can do something, doesn't he? So there must be plenty.'' He turned towards the door. ''I'll be seeing you.''

He reached the door.

''Jeff,'' called his father, quietly.

Lorna sensed that the tension was near breaking-point; and she sensed more. Saul Wannaker was used to command and his son was used to obedience – but there was a chance, a big chance, that he would revolt now.

He stopped, with a hand at the door.

If he opened it and went out, Lorna felt, there might be a bitter estrangement between father and son. It was all so near the surface; and somehow it mattered to her. She hoped that Jeff would turn round. She could see that his father wanted it. She couldn't be sure what Elaine was feeling behind that beautiful pink mask of a face.

Jeff turned, slowly.

"Jeff, listen to me," his father began. "I want you –"

"Dad, I don't want to quarrel with you," Jeff said quietly. "But I'm in this affair as deep as I can go. You haven't met Helen Chadwick, have you?"

His father didn't speak.

"Ever since I saw her, she's haunted me," Jeff said quietly. "She matters in the way that Elaine matters to you. I just have to go on."

12

## MANNERING WAKES

JOHN MANNERING heard a faint movement, as if a long way off, and lay waiting for it to come again. It didn't. He kept his eyes closed. His head ached, vaguely. His mind was hazy, and he was reluctant to make himself think although he knew that there was something unpleasant on his mind. In spite of the reputation that his past deeds had won for him, he was a human being with human failings; and just now his failing was unwillingness to face unwanted facts.

They crept into his mind.

He remembered why his head ached; remembered much of what had happened: remembered May Sharp with the gash in her neck. That was it: murder and a murderer to be found, with much responsibility on him because May had really been working for him.

He opened his eyes.

He was in bed, and it was dark. He could see the stars. Distant noises came from the streets but they were not the cause of his awakening. That had been a sound inside the flat. He waited for several more minutes, snug and warm, and persuaded himself that he now remembered everything that had happened, and should now be in better shape to do something about it.

He pushed the bedclothes back, and got out of bed. His head stood that test well. He switched on the bedside light, and then rinsed his hands and face in cold water. That made him feel almost human. He put on a dressing-gown and pushed his feet into slippers, then opened the door. There was no light on in the hall, but there was one in the kitchen and another in the study.

Then the study door opened, light flooded the hall and made him close his eyes against the glare.

"Darling!" exclaimed Lorna. "I looked in a minute ago and you were still asleep."

"Couldn't rest," said Mannering, in a solemn voice. "I just had to see you." He slid his arm round her waist, and they went into the study. She had been sewing; the basket of cottons and buttons, wools and oddments, was by her chair, a needle was stuck in the arm; and she wore horn-rimmed glasses. Solemnly, he kissed her. "How long have you been home?"

"Oh, hours. It's nearly nine. I'll tell Ethel to bring in your supper. You'd better have it in here."

She went out.

Mannering decided that he could risk a weak whisky-and-soda without fearing that it would go to his head.

He poured, and sipped. When Lorna came back, he was standing with the glass in one hand and a cigarette in the other.

"Who's been doing what?" he asked hopefully.

"I don't think anybody's been doing much," Lorna said, sitting down and plucking the needle out of the arm. She held it up to judge the length of cotton. "Bristow telephoned twice, and said there's nothing to report. Pip Stocker called, but hasn't discovered anything. Larraby telephoned from the shop, nothing needs your attention there. In fact," went on Lorna, picking up a white silk slip and plunging the needle into a lace trimming which had started to come undone, "since the attack on Elaine Wannaker, I don't think anything's *happened* at all."

She went on sewing.

Mannering sipped his drink and watched her in his favourite if unconsidered pose; with his head on one side.

"Talk," he ordered.

"Oh, didn't you know about that?" asked Lorna, and looked up, straight-faced. "I thought you were psychic when you were on a case, darling, I must have been reading the wrong newspapers. A man attacked Elaine as she was about to open the door of the apartment. I know. I was there."

Mannering put his glass down abruptly.

"That's a very different matter. If you start getting in the line of fire — "

"Oh, but honey, think of poor Elaine," breathed Lorna. "She was the intended victim, and just imagine how terrible it would be if she were to become a cold, cold corpse."

"Poor Saul Wannaker," said Mannering stonily.

"I think you're right about that," Lorna agreed, and told him what had happened. Before she finished, Ethel came in with an omelette, piping hot, and crisp

94

fried bacon. Mannering's eyes brightened. "You're much better," Lorna declared. "I can see that you'll soon be doing something to justify your reputation."

He grimaced at her.

"Saul wouldn't tell the police about the attack," added Lorna.

Mannering said slowly: "And what excuse did he give for that, poor thing?"

"Don't let the omelette get cold," said Lorna. "I'll talk, you can listen for once."

She finished her story.

Listening did not spoil the taste of the omelette for Mannering. He helped himself from a bowl of fruit salad, and said reflectively:

"Domestic scenes. Here, for one, and at the Wannaker's apartment for another. So that's the ostensible reason why Saul backed out—threats to his Dresden doll. I'm not really surprised about Jeff, although he seems to have been taken by love for Helen pretty suddenly. Still, it's happened before, and the whole family seems to be in a tense emotional state. What did you think of the set-up?"

"Jeff hates Elaine. Saul tries to steer an even course between them, and doesn't always find it easy."

"Your best nautical style," murmured Mannering, "but I see what you mean. And you dislike Elaine, too."

Lorna said slowly: "As a matter of fact, darling, I don't." She dropped the mood of semi-flippancy, and Mannering sensed the change. "I thought I was going to, but she rather improves on acquaintance. She isn't just an empty-headed butterfly, she can talk about painting, knows the different schools and isn't a bad judge. When she forgets herself, she's nice. It's when she's acting that I could spank her."

"Acting?"

"The way she behaves with men is one big act,"

95

Lorna said dryly. "I suppose that's all it is — the way she behaves with men."

"How does she feel towards Jeff?"

"She didn't give herself away. He came to the flat with me, wouldn't take no — he seemed to imagine that I would think I'd be attacked any minute. He was rather awkward about the family set-up, wished that they hadn't talked in front of me, I think. How old is he?"

"Twenty-seven."

"He's coy enough for twenty-one at times, and at others almost a man-of-the-world," Lorna reflected. "He told me one thing that will interest you, too."

"What?"

"Robbie Chadwick was fired because he made a pass at Elaine," Lorna announced matter-of-factedly. "Jeff thinks that she encouraged Robbie, and when they were caught, turned round and blamed him for getting fresh. It was almost a question of throwing Robbie Chadwick out."

"And giving him a motive to dislike the Wannakers," Mannering remarked thoughtfully. "We've some magnificent motives in this job. I've picked up a few other odds and ends, too. Saul Wannaker's buying up shares in all the companies which are going to have a dollar-transfusion to keep them healthy. Huge money's involved, and he could make millions. Would he lose a chance of that to save his sweetie pie? Or is he doing a deal for those missing details? Remember, anyone who gets in before he buys will make a big profit, and cut Saul's. That's the big end — the jewel robbery is just a side-line. Did Jeff tell you what he thinks about the robbery?"

"He's pretty sure it was Robbie," said Lorna, "but he doesn't want to think so, because Helen Chadwick has dazzled him."

"Her eyes," declared Mannering, firmly.

"Are they *so* wonderful?" Lorna was sceptical.

Mannering said gently: "My sweet, they are capable of making a sane man turn into a drooling fool. Empires have fallen and battles been fought for eyes like Helen Chadwick's. Yes, they're wonderful." He didn't smile, and she knew that he was in earnest. "She's quite a girl, and she's a prisoner of men who've already killed once. Why did they kill? Why should anyone want to murder Helen Chadwick, if it was a mistaken identity job? What comes first — the jewels, or the share business?" He stood up, quickly. "I don't get it, I don't like it, and —"

The telephone bell rang.

He answered it, moving briskly, telling himself that he hadn't anything much to worry about, his head would stand up to all normal usage.

"Hallo?"

"John," said Pip Stocker, "I think I know where Ben is, and who he is. Nicholas Bennett, with a house in St Johns Wood. Helen Chadwick and her brother might be there, too."


.    .    .


It was the news Mannering had been waiting for, the news which really mattered. Finding the jewels and finding if the markets were being played at Saul Wannaker's expense was important — but the Chadwicks mattered much more; especially Helen. He had buoyed her up with false hope, and he wanted to redeem himself.

"What's the address?" he asked softly.

Lorna stood up quickly.

". . . 103 Courtney Street," Mannering repeated into the telephone. "Thanks, Pip . . . Yes, in about two hours, I should say, but come yourself, I don't want any legmen . . . Thanks." He added 'goodbye', and rang off. He was smiling. He looked exactly as the portrait of the Cavalier — had the same curve of the lips, gave the impression that action was pending, that he could hardly wait to draw his sword from the scabbard.

"I'm going to have a word with Ben," he said, and Lorna knew that it would be useless to try to dissuade him, even by reminding him of the lump at the back of his head.

She saw him change in front of her eyes.

The years rolled back.

She saw him as he had been when they had first met; man-about-town, wealthy, handsome enough to stir the hearts of dowagers and hopeful debutantes, popular and highly respected – by day. And by night, she had discovered, he was a daring devil-may-care, swooping upon the homes of the wealthy, winning for himself a dazzling reputation as a jewel-thief who set the Press, the police and the public by the ears.

The Baron became a byword; a legend; a dream.

When she had first discovered it, she had hated the truth.

Then she learned how a woman had betrayed and embittered him, and how he seemed to seek revenge upon the women of beauty and wealth and high estate. But he was not a man in whom bitterness could live for long, there was too much of the glow of humour in him. Gradually, the bitterness had thawed, and from a cracksman who had learned every trick of the burglar's trade he had become what he was now – poacher turned gamekeeper, but still in the public eye.

Bristow had known him in his first guise, but had never been able to put him in dock.

Bristow knew much about the past, when the Press had dubbed Mannering the Baron, and the name had been blazoned on the headlines of newspapers in three continents. The Baron's record and his escapes from the law would always linger in Bristow's thoughts and tinge them with suspicion.

All this passed through Lorna's mind as she watched

Mannering, seeing the glint in his eyes, the lift of his head, the thrust of his chin. He was going to do battle. He had long been a kind of modern St George, setting himself to right wrongs, to rob the rich and help the poor – and to the devil with law and order. He really belonged to a bygone, swashbuckling age. Of the different portraits she had painted of him, the one at Quinns, in Cavalier's dress, was more truly the real man.

He leaned over her and kissed her.

"I'd think I'd better dress up," he said, "and make a fool of myself, as usual. Care to help?"

She knew that she would have to . . .

She helped, while he sat in front of the dressing-table, with a make-up case spread out, working on his face, using greasepaint with swift, subtle skill, to alter the look even of the bone formation; or using tiny pellets to broaden his nose; spirit gum at the corners of his eyes; a rubber covering over his fine white teeth; clippers at the back and sides of his hair.

In an hour, a different man stood up and looked at Lorna.

Ten minutes later still, he was dressed with a padded suit to make him look both stout and round-shouldered; and had a tool-kit wound about his waist containing everything needed to break open a door, or a safe, or even a strong-room.

"John," Lorna said, "don't take risks on your own. You needn't. Have Pip – "

"He'll be at hand," Mannering said. "That's a guarantee. He's anxious to show me that he's really good – this is the first big job we've worked together on, except that one in Paris last year. Pip's going places, and I'd like a stooge sometimes."

"Don't rely on him too much, don't even rely on yourself," Lorna said, and burst out: "I hate this whole business!"

Mannering didn't speak.

Lorna stood at the window of the drawing-room when he left, looking into Green Street and watching him walk towards the main road, King's Road, where he would take a bus or a taxi to Victoria, and go to a lock-up garage where he kept a car which he used for such jaunts as this.

He went with all the confidence in the world; she could imagine the excitement within him. He was going to find a killer and bring him to book, and everything but that was forgotten.

She was forgotten, too.

She watched him turn the corner. Her eyes were very bright. She lit a cigarette, then stared at a mirror, but for a few minutes saw nothing but a blur. She had often watched him go like this, with the courage and the daring which made so many men worship him; and each time she knew fear.

He might not come back.

Next time, his skull might be smashed.

These people were killers.

## 13

## THE QUIET HOUSE

MANNERING pulled up in the black Morris with a super-charged engine at a corner not far from Courtney Street. Street lamps burned. Two or three other cars were parked with their side lights on but no one walked along the road. He moved away, limping slightly, to make him look less like his real self. He had forgotten the past and all the motives for this sortie, save one: he wanted to avenge a murdered woman who had worked for him.

He turned into Courtney Street.

Here were two cars; and in the second, a bright green M.G., sat Pip Stocker.

Mannering passed, saying:

"Give me an hour, Pip, and then take a signal."

Stocker didn't speak, didn't even turn around. He had seen the man coming, watched him limp, seen his bulk, his rounded shoulders and his barrel-like torso, and been sure that this wasn't Mannering. But it had been Mannering's voice. Pip watched him receding in the driving mirror, and lit another cigarette.

Mannering turned a corner.

There was a light on inside the hall of Number 103. The number itself showed plainly against the frosted glass fanlight. There was a light at a first-floor window, too.

Mannering walked along, briskly.

He knew the type of houses well; three-storey, including the attic flat but not including the basement. There was a small garden in front of each and a long narrow garden at the back of each; but no approach to the back except through the house.

The windows were of the sash-cord type. The walls were thick and solid, sound wouldn't travel far inside them. Unless Nicholas Bennett had changed the locks and window fastenings, there would not be much difficulty getting in. A little square porch gave some shadow, too; unless a policeman passed while he was at the door, he would get inside without any risk of being seen.

He walked past, on the opposite side of the road, and then walked back. No one was about.

The light went out, and Number 103 was in darkness.

Mannering crossed the road.

The thrill of excitement merged with the caution of experience. He glanced swiftly up and down; the road was still deserted. It was nearly midnight, and there would be few people along now; there was hardly a light to be seen.

He looked at the iron gate, which was clearly visible in the lamplight; there were no attached wires, nothing to suggest that it was wired up to cause an alarm. He opened it cautiously; it moved easily and without difficulty. He stepped on to grass, and walked more briskly towards the front door. Once there he tied a blue scarf round his head, leaving only his eyes and forehead visible. He looked round to make sure that no one was in sight. Then he stepped into the porch, with a pen-knife in his hand, open to a skeleton key blade. He might not need the tool-kit. The tips of his fingers were covered with a thin, pliable plastic, a false skin to avoid leaving fingerprints.

The light was poor, here.

He switched on a pencil torch, and peered at the lock. It looked simple. He put the light out and thrust the skeleton key in, twisted and turned — and in a few seconds knew that appearances were false, this lock wouldn't be easy to force.

He drew the key out.

A special lock was a challenge. Inside it would have intrigued and even excited him, but he wanted to get into the house in a hurry. He knew all the risks. His ears were strained to catch the sound of heavy footsteps of a policeman on patrol; of the sound of a car; or of people hurrying to their homes, who might cast a casual glance towards this house and see him, and raise the alarm.

He put the knife away, and took a tool from the kit at his waist-band. His hands were steady, and his face was set in a smile. He thrust the tool into the lock, and began to work it with swift, dexterous movements; in a few seconds he knew that there was a chance.

He worked on.

The lock clicked.

That was a moment of triumph, like seeing a football go into the net, or the bails fly, or a horse flash past the post wearing the right colours and carrying the right man's money. Mannering turned the lock carefully, then withdrew the key. The door would be bolted, too, but he could tackle that next. There might be a chain, too.

He thrust at the door, and it did not yield.

Then he heard a car engine, and headlights flashed into the black night as a car turned into the street. Mannering moved, swiftly. The driver would not see him, and no passenger was likely to, but if the car were coming here, he must get out of the way.

The car passed, with darkness following the trail of its headlamps.

Mannering went back to the porch, and took out a thin steel tool, thrust it between the door and the frame, and found the flange but nothing to suggest an alarm wire. He pushed harder, and the point of the tool went into the wood and, as he twisted, through it. Then he used a saw with a pointed end. After the first few seconds, the teeth began to cut. He cut through the flange without much trouble and came to the top bolt; this needed a different saw. He withdrew the other, oiled a blade of a tiny hacksaw, and put it in position.

In spite of the oil, metal scraping on metal made a harsh, hurtful sound; it set his teeth on edge, and started his heart thumping, but he didn't stop. His ears were strained more tensely now to catch sounds above the one that he was making. Every few seconds he stopped, to listen; and had to allow the echo of this sound to fade before he could be sure that no one was approaching.

He heard a motor-cycle engine.

He remembered Lorna's story of a runaway motor-cyclist.

He snatched the saw out, and thrust it into his pocket as he moved out of the porch and towards the side of the house, where the shadow would hide him. But if the motor-cyclist were coming here, the fact that the door was sawn through would be discovered, and —

The motor-cycle passed.

Mannering felt the relief melt his tension. It was always the same; never a moment when he could relax or be indifferent to the dangers of forcing entry. For if he were caught and the Chadwicks were not here and there was no evidence against Ben —

He thrust the thought out of his mind, and started to go back, then stopped again. A man walked steadily, heavily, along the road. A torch flashed; this was the policeman on his round. Mannering was glad to see his helmet above the garden wall, to know that there would be no danger from the police once this man had passed.

The helmet moved along steadily, going up and down with the policeman's movements; and then the big body passed the iron gates, and the man disappeared. Mannering waited for another half-minute, then went back to the door; but he still hesitated. The police were trained to have sharp ears; the sound of metal sawing on metal might travel a long way in the night's quiet.

He waited for five minutes, then began again.

The movement was slow and laborious, there was no way of being sure that the teeth were cutting; it was like having faith. It was nerve-wracking, too, because he had to pause to listen so often; but it would be crazy to take chances, success depended on extreme caution.

He felt the resistance slacken, and his heart began to thump. He sawed gently, and the blade met no resistance. The top bolt was through, and with luck there wasn't one at the bottom.

He thrust at the door.

It opened.

He stepped into the dark, quiet house.

. . .

Houses had atmosphere, especially by night. Closing
the door with the same stealth as the Baron in days of
old, but leaving it unlatched so that he could get out
quickly in an emergency, Mannering stepped towards
the foot of the stairs, his feeling for the Baron's past
almost nostalgic.

There was the slightly astringent smell of distemper;
so the hall had recently been colour-washed. It showed
up pale, ghostly. A smell of polish suggested a house-
proud woman. There was also a faint smell of paint; so
the tenants were probably new – or Spring cleaning had
been very thorough.

He shone his torch.

Its narrow beam shone on the stairs, the narrow strip
of carpet which ran up them, on the pale walls and the
shiny banisters and the big newel post at the bottom.
There was silence everywhere; but silence could be
treacherous, and it did not mean that everyone was
asleep.

He checked the rooms; two led to the left, there was
another at the end of the staircase, probably one
beyond that. He walked softly, with a felt pad over his
soles; and he made no sound as he opened door after
door, making sure that each room was empty.

In the kitchen, a table was laid for breakfast, with
a big packet of cereals on it; sugar; a silver toast rack.
The little touch was so normal that it was easy to
believe that Stocker was wrong. A woman's green
plastic apron hung behind the door; a few oddments
had a nice, homely touch. He frowned as he turned
out of the stairs.

He kept close to the side, an old trick to avoid

making the stairs creak; but one creaked loudly. He reached the landing.

He thought he heard a noise.

A car moved along a nearby street and he could hear the engine, but the sound that had made him stop seemed to be much nearer. He didn't move. The sound wasn't repeated. He relaxed, and went forward slowly, but was more alert than he had been and his heart was thumping noisily; he could do this a thousand times, and not get used to it.

He checked the doors on this floor; five. Bathroom and W.C. – and that left three. Each was unlocked.

He put out the torch, and opened a door opposite the head of the stairs. It creaked slightly, and he caught his breath, but nothing else moved. In the back of his mind was nervousness because of that imagined noise, but he could only go on.

He heard breathing.

Lamplight came through the window, and Mannering was able to make out the shape of the room, the pale walls, the twin beds. A man and a woman lay sleeping. He went nearer. The man was closer to the tall windows. His hair was dark, and he had a bald patch.

Was it Ben? Nicholas Bennett?

Mannering drew nearer. He didn't want to use the torch, light in the sleeping man's eyes would probably rouse him. A yard from the bed, he stopped.

He looked like Ben – if Helen had described him accurately.

The woman had her back to Mannering.

He went nearer. She had brassy hair, and was snuggled well beneath the bedclothes, with nothing showing but her head. She breathed evenly and heavily.

Mannering went out.

He stood by the door, listening for any change in the man's breathing but heard none. He closed the door, without making a sound. He felt sure in his heart that the sleeping man was Ben, but he hadn't expected a woman. Wife?

He tried the handle of the next door. It opened at once, and the breathing he heard here was heavier. There was more light from a lamp almost outside the window.

Mannering drew nearer.

This was Lanky Dan with the wiry hair and the sneer, the man who had stepped out of the wardrobe at May Sharp's body. So Stocker was right, and this was the household. Was Percy Morino here, too? Were the Chadwicks?

Hope set Mannering's heart thumping. He turned away, went through all the routine again, closed the door and approached the next room.

It was a library, with books lining two walls, a big desk, several small tables; nothing was really unusual. There was a smell of pipe tobacco smoke, and on the table a tray with whisky and a syphon of soda and one empty glass.

What of the next floor?

If the Chadwicks were here, they would almost certainly be up there. He ought to find that out first and go through the papers in this room afterwards. Yet the temptation to search here first was almost overwhelming; so were the arguments. If he could find evidence against Ben, it would help the Chadwicks vitally. Once they were free from Ben, they would have the police to face, so — find the evidence to help them first.

It might be here.

He actually stepped towards the desk, then reminded himself that he must check every room, make sure that he knew all the odds, before he started searching. So he walked across the room, the felt on his shoes dragging on the thick pile of the carpet. He stepped outside.

He heard the sound again; of a creaking door.

# 14

## STRUGGLE

Mannering stood still, tense.

The creaking sound came again, and he was quite sure that it was a door; and that it was made stealthily. He saw no one and nothing appeared to move. He stood with his back against the dark wood — the wall itself was light and would reveal him.

A shuffling sound followed.

Whoever it was would probably have a gun, and wasn't likely to hesitate to use it. Mannering was a sitting bird; being found here would damn him in the eyes of the police.

A floorboard creaked, and Mannering saw faint light coming from the room where he had seen Lanky Dan. The street lamp outside cast a glow which opened further as Lanky Dan opened the door.

A shadow appeared, vague and ill-formed.

Mannering did not move.

Lanky Dan appeared, just a shape — a tall silhouette against the wall. Bless that pale distemper! Would he come this way, trying to find out what was happening by himself? Or would he first raise an alarm?

Mannering dared hardly breathe.

Lanky Dan's breath whistled slightly.

If he turned right, towards Ben's bedroom, then Mannering would have to swing into action. If he came this way, Mannering could wait for a chance to grab him by the throat. Would he disturb Ben, his boss, unless he were sure that there was trouble?

There was an agonising minute of uncertainty, before Dan turned this way. He was caught in the brightest light, and his hands and face showed; the gun in his right hand had a short, stubby snout.

Mannering put a hand to his pocket, gripped a length of rubber tubing, and dared hardly draw it out for fear of making a sound. The other man came towards him. The room was at the end of the passage which ran along the stairs, opposite the foot of the next flight of stairs.

Lanky Dan was peering ahead, as if trying to pierce the gloom. Mannering's face was covered with the blue scarf, his hands were out of sight and nothing light would show up; but some men had uncanny eyesight.

Dan drew nearer.

Mannering could not see the gun, now; and if this man saw or even thought he saw a movement, he would shoot first and worry afterwards. It was impossible to see the trigger-finger, to have the slightest warning. Mannering breathed so softly that it was hardly like breathing. The only sounds were the faint rustling of Dan's approach, and the faint whistling of his breath.

He was only three yards away; soon, he would be within striking distance.

Soon —

He could shoot and kill.

He drew nearer. There was no shred of doubt about his stealth; his determination not to be heard. Why? Did he suspect a burglar; or did he think that someone in the house was on the prowl; or was he on some secret errand?

Mannering almost stopped breathing.

He could hear the whistle of the other man's breath clearly. He held the rubber-tubing loosely, ready to tighten his grip any second, but a snatch at the throat, to choke the inevitable cry, was better by far.

Nearer —

A light went on, behind Dan.

·   ·   ·

The light was brilliant where it came through an open

door. Dan swung round. Mannering saw a shadow on the landing, and knew that Ben would soon be here. Ben could not fail to see him. He had a split second to decide in, and pushed the study door open and stepped inside.

"And what's given you insomnia?" Ben asked, in a nasty voice.

Mannering couldn't see either of the men, but moved slowly, fearfully, until he was behind the crack of the door. Now he could see them both – Ben was coming forward. Neither of them could have any idea that he was near.

"Gone deaf, too?" sneered Ben.

"I – I heard something," Lanky Dan protested. He didn't sound happy; there was no shadow of doubt that Ben was the boss. "I *thought* I heard something."

That sounded so lame that even Mannering doubted him.

"When I hear anything, I hear it," Ben said, and Mannering could understand why his voice caused alarm and anxiety. "You were going to snoop around, Dan. Why is that? Don't you trust me?"

"Ben, it isn't true, I – "

"So you were just sleep-walking," Ben murmured. "Sleep-walking or suffering from insomnia or curiosity *or* getting greedy. Which *was* it, Dan?"

"Ben, I swear – "

"Listen, Dan," said Ben softly, menacingly. "I wouldn't believe anything you said even if you were to swear it on the Bible, see. Not even if you were to give evidence under oath, I wouldn't believe you. Have you been into that room?"

"No!"

"Well," said Ben, "the door's open. Doors don't open by themselves."

"I tell you I heard something! I came out to find out what it was."

"Dan, I'm grown up," Ben said nastily. "Didn't anyone tell you that? I wasn't born yesterday, Danny Boy. I don't trust you. You've been in there, you've heard me coming and you tried to make it look as if you were going, not coming. And that's how it happened."

Dan was breathless; as if terrified.

"No, Ben, it wasn't! Ben, listen — "

They were out of sight, now, and only a yard from the door. Mannering had the tubing in his hand, but a length of rubber-tubing would not be much good against two armed men. This light would go on in a moment, and once that happened he would be seen. He saw the door open wider, then saw the hand come into the room, groping for the light.

He smashed the tubing on to the hand, and as it struck and the victim gasped in pain, he pulled the door wide open. In that split second, he saw Ben snatching his injured hand away, Dan with the gun lowered and gaping, mouth wide open, all his teeth showing.

Mannering leapt and struck. One false move, one second wasted, and he would have lost his chance. He caught Dan on the side of the chin, and Dan fell sideways. The gun dropped. Dan struck the wall heavily and his hands scrabbled at it, he began to slither down.

Mannering bent down, snatched up the gun, and spun round. Ben showed up in the light which came from his bedroom. He was snatching at his right-hand pocket with his left hand, and holding his right hand up, as if he couldn't use it. His round face had an evil look, and his eyes had beastliness burning in them.

Mannering raised his right leg and drove his foot into Ben's stomach. He heard the wind belch out. Ben staggered back, eyes rolling. The door banged back loudly, too loudly. Ben crumpled up, his knees bending. He swayed in a foolish way, to and fro, to and fro, mouth opening wide. Mannering turned the gun in his right hand and struck Ben on the side of the head, and turned again. He needed luck, and he was getting the luck. Dan was mouthing, but the blow must have struck a nerve centre, he couldn't control himself, was writhing on the floor. Mannering used the gun as a cosh again.

The man stopped moving.

Mannering stood quite still. Sweat beaded his forehead, and was cold on the back of his neck. Two men lay unconscious, where he might have been laying dead. The fear of death gave him strength no one would possess without it. He felt weak, exhausted. His head was beginning to ache again.

He watched the lighted bedroom.

Nothing stirred.

Had the woman slept through this? The thudding, the gasping and the banging door?

Still nothing moved.

Mannering took a handkerchief from his pocket and dabbed his forehead and his neck. First things first. He took a coil of cord from his tool-kit, and bent over Dan; it took him less than a minute to tie Dan's hands and ankles together, gag him, and drag him into the study. He did the same with Ben. All the time he watched Ben's bedroom door.

No shadow appeared and nothing moved.

Mannering began to smile, with a tension which the Baron had known so often; tension which was touched with exhilaration. He'd won out; at least, he was winning. There might be others, but he wasn't likely to be caught napping. Boldness paid, as always.

He seemed to stand outside himself, and call a warning; this was the moment of greatest danger because of over-confidence.

He steadied.

He moved towards the bedroom. He would have to bind and gag the woman, he dared not take a chance that she would wake up and find the other bed empty. Amazing that the light and the banging hadn't disturbed her; call it lucky night indeed. Virtue carried its own reward. Careful, that was a silly mood, one likely to induce carelessness.

He crept into the bedroom.

The woman wasn't there.

.　　.　　.

Mannering stared at the empty bed, the turned back sheets and blankets, the pillow where the woman's head had been. He couldn't believe it, but this was true. Then he understood why, and his mind began to work again. A wardrobe door stood open. He had been fooled by a man in a wardrobe before. He covered the door with the gun, and said very softly:

"Come out."

There was no response.

"Come out," he repeated. "I won't hurt you if you come at once."

The woman didn't answer.

"Listen," Mannering said, "you'll get hurt if you stall any longer. Come out, and keep your hands in sight. Ben and Dan are — "

"Just drop that gun and put your hands up," a woman said from the doorway behind him.

15

BEN'S WIFE

MANNERING did not move, but his grip on the gun tightened. After the first flash of alarm, he understood what had happened. There was a door behind the wardrobe. The woman had gone into another room through that, and kept in hiding until able to get behind him.

She might not have a gun.

"Or *you'll* get hurt," she said, and he thought that she came a step nearer. She wasn't like a man, wouldn't know the tricks; would she? He kept the gun in his hand.

"Listen," he began again, "I won't hurt—"

He heard a funny little sneezing sound, then a roar of a shot. A hole appeared in the door of the wardrobe, which swung to, violently. He didn't question her gun or the woman's mood any longer, and she had the edge. The door was quivering and the sound echoing when he turned round and tossed his gun into her face.

She was a blonde, short, plumpish, wearing yellow pyjamas which weren't fastened properly at the breast. She had her gun in her right hand, but made a convulsive movement to escape Mannering's. He jumped at her. She tried to bring her gun to bear, but he caught her right wrist and wrenched it, and the gun dropped.

It went off.

He felt nothing.

The woman struck at him with her free hand, for a moment they were close together, her billowy softness against his padded weight. One moment she was straining every muscle and every nerve; the next she would have fallen if Mannering hadn't kept an arm round her shoulder. She didn't faint or close her eyes, just went limp.

.   .   .

The crisis had passed, he could breathe again.

.   .   .

He carried her to the bed and put her on it, flat on her back.

"Don't take it the hard way," Mannering said, and took out the cord. He made a loop, grabbed her wrists and slipped the loop over, then drew it tight but not tight enough to hurt.

Her eyes weren't really frightened — not terrified, as a woman's might have been expected to be.

"I won't hurt you," Mannering said. "Just take it easy."

"What do you want?" Her husky voice was surprisingly steady, her gaze was steady, too. She stared as if searching for something.

"I want a talk with Ben when he wakes up, and a look through his study," Mannering said. "Forget it." He tied another loop round her ankles. Her feet were small and very white except for a tracery of tiny blue veins, and she had nice ankles and well-shaped legs. She was looking at him as if she wanted him to appreciate that. "Who else is in the house?" Mannering demanded.

"There's that blue-eyed doll," she said. "Is that who you've come for?"

. . .

Mannering didn't slacken the cord, just tightened it round the woman's ankles. But his heart began the old tricks again, thumping heavily; he was close to complete success because Helen was here. Who else could she mean?

"Where is she?"

"In the attic."

"Anyone else?"

"They took the man away before the girl got here," she said. "Listen, I'll play it your way, you needn't put that thing on me." She looked at the cloth which

Mannering took from his pocket, knowing that it was a gag. "I'll give you any help I can, I don't want more trouble."

"Neither of us wants any trouble," Mannering said. "Where does Ben keep his keys?"

She looked at him in a way he didn't like, in much the same way that Ben would look at someone he hated – but it wasn't so strong as that. Then she gave a little smile which might have been a sneer, and said:

"Chained to the bed, big boy."

He glanced at Ben's bed. A slim steel chain was fastened round one of the posts, and he stretched over and pulled at it; there were keys on a key-ring at the end. The chain had a patent fastening, and he forced it, then slid the keys into his pocket. They made quite a heavy weight.

"What do you expect to find?" the woman asked.

"Oh, a couple of fortunes," Mannering said. He wasn't thinking about her, but about Helen Chadwick. Where should he go first, to the attic or to the study? He had the keys, he could get the search over quickly, and then release Helen; if she were released first, she might make difficulties, certainly she would be desperately anxious to get away. In a way she would needle him, he might get impatient, careless.

The night had run well; he would try the study first.

He took out the keys.

"Which is the key to the safe?" he asked abruptly.

The woman hesitated again. She was nice to look at, and had a pleasant, open face with full lips. Because she had on no make-up, she looked wholesome. The only thing he didn't like about her was the expression in her eyes.

"Come on, answer," he said, sharply. He hadn't used pressure; he didn't want to hurt her, but if it were necessary he would.

"Those two big ones," she said. "If my hands were free – "

"They're not. Go on."

She shrugged; a wriggling kind of movement which took her further down the bed. He still didn't like the expression in her eyes, which were green-grey, good, rather bold. He wished he knew why he was so dubious about that look.

"Okay," she said, "the big brass one, and the one with the broken loop."

He identified the two keys easily, and was confident that they were the right ones. She knew that he would find them, so there was no point in her lying. But she behaved almost as if she had fooled him. Her expression was rather like the tone of Ben's voice; suggestive of evil things.

Was he dreaming this up?

There were the keys, and the safe was in the next room. This would be easy. He glanced at a strap-watch, one which he kept in the secret car. He had another half-hour before Stocker was due.

"Head up," he said, and held out the cloth.

She submitted tamely, and he put the cloth round the back of her head – and then she bit him. Her teeth buried themselves in the fleshy heel of his left hand. He winced, and snatched his hand free. The pain made him hold his breath, and blood welled up from the white marks of her teeth. Her eyes blazed at him, there was a kind of laughter in them, as if that was what she had meant to do from the beginning; it might explain the look in her eyes.

He straightened up, and grinned down at her; showing the ugly yellow teeth, knowing that if she saw him without the disguise, next day, even within the next hour, she would never recognise him.

"That was silly," he said, "don't do it any more."

He gagged her, and she didn't bite again. Her eyes

were still glittering when he went out of the room, with the keys in his hand. He couldn't be sure that she had told the truth, there might be others in the house, he ought to look round first. He changed his mind about going straight to the study, and hurried up the stairs.

There were three rooms and a boxroom on the attic floor, and the first two rooms he looked in had sloping ceilings. The third was the boxroom. He had only the fourth to visit, and the door was locked; so Helen would be in here.

He didn't waste time trying to find the key on Ben's ring, but used a skeleton key, forced the lock, thrust the door open and stepped inside.

This room was empty, too.

There were some clothes, Helen Chadwick's clothes, with American tabs; that was all.

.     .     .

The woman looked at him defiantly. She didn't lack courage; she probably didn't lack anything except her share of goodness. The gag was loose over her chin, but she knew that Mannering would tighten it as soon as he had finished.

The light glinted on a golden wedding ring.

"I thought she was still there," she said, "*I* didn't see her go."

"When did you last see her?"

"Dinner time. About eight o'clock, I suppose, I took her some food. It was a damned sight better than she deserved, the — "

"Was she all right?"

"No one had assaulted her, if *that's* what you mean."

Mannering pulled the gag into position and tightened it. The greeny-grey eyes glared at him. He turned away, feeling sick at the thought that he had come too late.

Where was Helen now?

Ben would know; but Mannering couldn't stay here much longer, there wasn't time to try to make him talk. He could take Ben away, but – where to?

He went downstairs and opened the front door cautiously. He went into the street, waited until his watch said two, then shone his torch, twice. An answering signal came from Stocker. He went back to the house. Stocker would wait all night if need be, but it was getting near danger point. One could trust the fates too far. Mannering was beginning to feel on edge; heard sounds which were not made, saw shadows which were not on the wall. The disappointment had been very sharp.

He moved towards the bedroom, passed the door, and turned back. He switched on the light. The woman lay and looked at him, balefully. She could hardly move, yet she managed to throw insults and sneers at him. The uneasiness turned into disquiet. There was something here that he did not know about, some danger which she knew existed and of which she hadn't warned him.

He put out the light and went to the study.

He seemed to see Helen Chadwick's eyes, in the darkness of the room. They were so beautiful that he could remember everything about them; their brightness and the glow of fear in them – and the relief when she had believed that he could help. He remembered telling Lorna what he thought about those eyes; what any man would have to think. Did thought of Helen Chadwick affect him more than it should?

She had obsessed Jeff Wannaker almost on sight.

But – had she? Or had Jeff used that as an excuse to go on looking for the jewels and the papers, and for forcing a clash with his father? Why did Jeff dislike his step-mother so much? Was it just family dislike, jealousy, the thwarting of a father and son relationship?

He shouldn't be thinking of these things; he ought to concentrate on the job in hand. He had one worry, now –finding what was in the safe, looking for evidence. He might never have another chance, he had to see it through. There was a lot at stake. He was working for the safety of Helen Chadwick; seeking the truth about Robbie Chadwick; and looking for Dizzy.

Dizzy was a name known to the police of three continents – as a fence, as a criminal who made ordinary crooks look like pygmies. Dizzy had become a byword in the world of crime and that borderland where criminals lived uneasily, and mixed with men of good faith. Among jewel collectors, connoisseurs, dealers; among everyone who had a love of precious stones and *objects d'art* and things of great beauty. Dizzy was a name and a reputation, as evil in his day as the reputation of the Baron had been romantic in his.

Dizzy was like a dark shadow, compelling others to take on the substance of crime, and there was good reason to believe that Ben, Lanky Dan, this mob, were really working for Dizzy. The police could not reach him, hard though they tried; he had avoided a clash. But, six months ago, he and the Baron had met head-on. As a result, some of those who had served Dizzy, knowing only his soubriquet and being hardly sure of his existence, were being entertained in Her Majesty's jails. Others, who had escaped the law but not the lash of the Baron's tongue nor dread of his vengeance, lived in mingled fear and hatred of the Baron.

Mannering knew these things, knew of Dizzy but did not know who he was.

All this nagged at him as he looked at Dan, who was still unconscious; and at Ben, whose eyes were open and held the same expression as in those of the woman –his wife? Well, why not? The gag at Ben's mouth was still very tight, and his bonds were much tighter than the woman's.

Mannering unfastened the gag.

"Where's Helen Chadwick?" he asked, harshly.

Ben sneered:

"You'd like to know. I—"

He flinched as Mannering struck him; but he didn't talk. Nothing short of torture would make him. His face was beaded with sweat when Mannering gave up trying to make him talk, but there was a glitter of satisfaction in his eyes.

Mannering tied the gag again.

"I'm coming for you again," he said.

He lifted the keys, selecting the two which the woman had pointed out. He was still looking at Ben. He saw the glint in Ben's eyes; almost like the fiery dart of light which would spring from a diamond suddenly exposed to it. His uneasiness became disquiet, became something near alarm. It was as if the helpless pair believed they could fool him. He went towards the safe. He glanced round at Ben again, but saw nothing odd now; had that been imagination?

He examined the safe thoroughly, but could not forget the eyes of the man behind him, or the menace which seemed to have shown in both Ben and the woman; the sneering, gloating expression.

The safe was a new Landon, the nearest thing to a perfect job. Without the keys, Mannering could not have opened it with tools, would have been forced to blow it. But the two keys should make all the difference. Were they right? He glanced down at them, and then at the safe. There were trick-safes by the dozen; by the hundred. There were safes which, when opened, spat a lethal bullet at the man standing in front of it; or spat fire; or gas. There were safes which were deadly containers of powerful current which would kill a man at a touch.

This looked harmless; but they all did.

Sometimes the turning of the first key started the mechanism, or switched on the current.

He inserted the key.

He was more than ever conscious of the gaze of the man behind him, but did not turn round, did not want to let Ben think that he was even slightly nervous.

He kept to one side, out of the range of anything which might spit at him, and then pulled on a glove with a backing of asbestos. He inserted the key, very carefully; and turned it slowly. He heard the faint *click!* through the silence, the only sound. He opened the tiny door which had been unlocked, and which enabled him to insert the second key.

Nothing had gone wrong.

His imagination must have been working overtime.

He thrust in the second key, very slowly, using just as much caution. Fearful.

Still keeping to one side, holding his breath, he began to turn it. He felt no unusual pressure, nothing but the recollection of the way Ben and the woman had looked at him suggested that there might be anything wrong. He was ready to laugh at his own fears.

He felt a jolt.

The floor gave way beneath him and he went hurtling into darkness.


16


## THE CELLAR


IN the split second as he fell it was as if Mannering were dropping to eternity. There was no time to try to save himself, to clutch at the edge of the floor. He just dropped. Then his mind worked, and he bent his knees, flexing his legs just before he struck the ground. The fall jarred him, but did no serious damage. He banged one knee on something hard, and pain shot through him; he heard the gasp forced from his lips.

Then he fell again, sideways.

Falling he struck the back of his skull. Pain greater than he had ever known streaked through his head, he could have screamed with it. In that moment of nightmare, it was as if he had screamed, was still screaming, and at the same time lifting his scalp from his head.

He lay in helpless torment.

Gradually, the pain eased. He had no idea how long he had lain there. The darkness had faded, now; faint light came from above him. He moved cautiously, and although his head throbbed, it wasn't unbearable. He moved his legs; one knee hurt a little, nothing was seriously wrong. He was alive, not badly hurt, a prisoner in darkness – and yet all about him he seemed to see the gloating eyes of the two people who had warned him.

He could imagine Ben laughing.

But Ben was helpless upstairs, with Lanky Dan near him, and the woman tied to the bed. There was still time to get away.

He stood up. His head seemed to swell and then contract, swell and contract; but soon, that steadied. He took out his pencil torch. The slim beam seemed very bright. It showed up against two walls, a vivid white ball about the size of a saucer; but in the other two directions it shot a long way across this room, and the light was diffused.

It shone on the stone steps leading up from the cellar; and, on the wall nearby, an electric light. He went across, narrowed his eyes, and switched on. The light began flickering from fluorescent strips; gradually it steadied. He had to wait to get used to it before he was able to look about him.

He didn't like what he saw.

The stone stairs led to a heavy steel door, and he could see the hinges were oiled, needing no telling that it was bolted from the other side; there was only one other way out — through the trap-door above.

He went down. The cellar was fairly clean. In one corner were sacks of a proprietary brand of coal; stacks of wood; the usual household oddments which had to be tucked away out of sight. Against one wall was a carpenter's bench; and when he got closer he saw that it was much more than that.

He began to whistle, softly.

This was a carpenter's shop and a tool-maker's bench in one. Here were hundreds of keys, which could be altered to fit a great variety of locks; all the tools needed to make keys. Here were the specialised tools a cracksman needed, far more than he carried round his waist.

His whistling grew more shrill.

The need to get out pressed less heavily on his mind for those few seconds. This was a discovery which would do Bristow a world of good. It was a kind of training school for cracksmen. He opened the doors of steel cupboards fastened to the wall above the bench, and found high explosives in tiny containers, all marked. There was nitro-glycerine in small plastic phials, each plainly marked: *Keep Very Steady*. And there were hand-grenades, coshes, jemmies; everything that a small army of burglars would need for massed raids.

He turned away.

The brief respite from acute anxiety brought fears back as sharply as ever.

The only way out was to blow the steel door, and that would almost certainly arouse the neighbours: the police would be here before he could shout.

He pulled a trestle from the wall by the logs; it was used for sawing the wood. Standing on it, he could just touch the trap-door. There was no handle on the inside, no way in which he could get a hold. He took out his tools and tried to prise the two halves of the trap-door open, but they would not budge. Electrically controlled, once they had closed, they could only be opened by the touch of a switch; or by cutting off the current.

The main switch wasn't here.

The only way he could get out was to blow the steel door at the head of the stairs. He could use nitro-glycerine there; he would have to. But he couldn't use it on the trap-door because the explosion might kill the men in the room above.

He took a phial from a cupboard and went towards the stairs. He tore a strip off a piece of cellulose tape, and fastened the nitro-glycerine container to the door. If he dropped it, and it went off before he was ready, it might blow him to pieces.

It stuck firmly.

He stood at the foot of the stairs, hesitating. Once it blew, there would probably be the alarm from neighbours – it wasn't absolutely certain but probable. He would have to get out, and forget the safe, forget evidence against Dizzy. But he could send the police here, if they arrived they would find the cellar full of cracksmen's tools, they wouldn't worry much about who had raided the place.

He went to the cellar, picked up several of the little ovals of coal, came back to the foot of the stairs, hesitated, and then tossed an oval at the steel door. He ducked behind the wall, heart in mouth; but the oval missed and clattered back to the floor.

He tried again – and dodged as swiftly. Once he struck the phial, the explosion would blast everything in its path.

He threw a third time.

He dived out of the way and flung himself flat, knowing that he wasn't going to miss. As he hit the floor, the explosion and the flash of flame came almost simultaneously, he was lifted off the floor and flung several feet away. The din deafened him and the pain at his head came back, he wanted to screech and scream again.

Then, gradually, the echo faded.

He got up.

Smoke and dust were billowing about the cellar, and he began to cough: coughing was agony, but he couldn't stop himself. He reached the head of the stairs. The swirling clouds almost hid the steel door from him, but at last he saw that a great hole had been ripped in it.

He went up, swiftly.

He heard nothing except the echoing in his ears. He reached a kitchen, with the back door fastened and bolted. He couldn't get out through the back garden except over the roof — wrong, he could climb wall after wall, if necessary. Anyone who came would come from the street.

He unlocked the door and stepped outside.

A light was on at a window of the house next door; and he saw moving shadows against the blind. He stepped slowly towards a little outhouse, and waited; and after five minutes, the light went out.

He went back into the house, and through the hall passage alongside the stairs, to the front door. He heard nothing. He opened it cautiously.

A man was coming from the gate.

.        .        .

Mannering saw the man, half turned, felt the desperation of defeat, and stopped moving. He hadn't been seen; he would wait, pounce on the man as he had pounced on Ben.

Then he saw that it was Stocker.

.　　　　.　　　　.

"All clear, Pip," Mannering whispered.

Stocker stopped abruptly.

"You all right?" He was straining his eyes to see Mannering against the dark front door.

"Fine."

"I heard a hell of an explosion."

"Nothing to worry about."

"Sure?"

"Yes."

"Finished?"

"Nearly," Mannering said. "I came to see if anyone had come to investigate. See any lights on?"

"No, but—"

"I won't be long now," Mannering said. "Keep watch."

"You've been a hell of a long time," Stocker grumbled. "And someone may have heard the bang and 'phoned the police."

"There'd be a light on. Give me twenty minutes."

"Oh, all right," Stocker conceded. "But if anyone else was worried by that explosion, there'll be trouble."

"You make yourself scarce, if you like," Mannering suggested.

"What the hell do you take me for?"

Mannering grinned in the darkness. "Sorry," he said and turned back into the house.

It looked as if his luck would hold. He did not need to put on a light to find the room where Ben and Dan were lying. He didn't trouble to look in the bedroom. Both men were awake, and when Ben saw him come in, he started so violently that he must have made the cords cut into his flesh.

Mannering gave him a mock salute.

"Now we'll really see what we can find," he said.

He went to the safe, kept clear of the trap-door, which was cunningly concealed by the pattern of the carpet, and turned the key which was still in the lock. The trap-door opened again; then closed. Smoke curled up from below. Mannering gave the key another turn, and heard the lock of the safe click open.

There might still be a trap.

He pulled the door open. It was very heavy, and hard to move. He stood behind it, but nothing spat at him, there seemed no need to worry.

There were jewel cases; documents; several wads of one pound notes, two of five pound notes. He took these out, piling them on the floor by his side. The Wannaker jewels weren't there. He looked quickly through the documents. Most were share certificates, many of them gilt-edged. Then he found a list of names and addresses, and Wannaker's name was on the list. Five minutes' search told him that he'd found the documents Wannaker had lost.

He put them in his pocket.

Next he found several small books, filled with notes, names and addresses, many of them of highly placed Government officials, big names in industry, banking, commerce. It looked as if someone had big plans for a financial coup.

He found nothing that pointed directly to any individual as the thief. Nothing to help identify Dizzy.

He hurried to the bedroom, where the woman lay with her eyes wide open, and the hatred in them gave an idea of what she would do if she were free. He grinned at her, picked up a suit-case from the top of the wardrobe, and went out. He filled the suit-case with the money and the jewel-cases.

"I'll leave the keys, Ben," he said amiably. "I hope they let you take them to jug with you! I'll be back!" He gave his mock salute again, and went out. The case was heavy. The one real anxiety was his failure to find Helen Chadwick and her brother.

He left the case in the hall and went to the stairs. Dan would talk more easily than Ben, but Ben probably knew more. He ought to take both of them away, but he mustn't run it too close. Ben or Dan?

He stood on the stairs, trying to decide, working out the details of getting a man away. A few minutes spent now might make the difference between success and failure.

It must be Ben, and—

Then he heard a police whistle.

## 17

## CHASE

MANNERING was on the move while the blast of the whistle still sounded. It came from the street, and couldn't be mistaken. He raced down the stairs. The suit-case was in his way, and the door was closed. He grabbed the case and opened the door wide — and saw a policeman coming towards him. He heard another blast of the whistle. If he were to get away, this was the moment.

He raced towards the policeman.

"Stop, there! Stop, or—"

Mannering ran on. The policeman grabbed wildly, then started another blast on the whistle. Mannering struck him on the side of the head, but the man stuck out a leg. Mannering stumbled. He felt a heavy blow in the face, and was pushed off his balance. The whistle shrilled again, and the policeman cracked a blow at Mannering's chin. Mannering swayed, slipped the punch, and brought his left fist up into the policeman's chin.

The blow connected; the man toppled backwards.

Mannering grabbed the case and raced towards the gate. Where the hell was Stocker? This was the moment he needed Stocker. He reached the gate.

"Turn right," Stocker said, gruffly. "Next corner."

Mannering turned. The case was heavy, his left knee hurt, he was afraid that his leg would give way. Stocker drew ahead. Lights were going up at windows — and a front door opened, a torch flashed out, a man cried:

"Here!"

Stocker was pounding away, Mannering forced himself to make another great effort. Another door opened, and someone shouted:

*"Thief, stop thief!"*

Now several men were running after Mannering. He could hear them. He was ten yards behind Stocker, and the others were close to him. The suit-case was so heavy, he ought to drop it; but he held on, he didn't know what would be in it. He felt a blow on the back of the head, but it wasn't heavy. He glanced round. One man was within twenty yards of him, drawing back an arm. Mannering didn't see what he threw, but heard it strike the pavement noisily.

Stocker turned the corner.

A police whistle shrilled out and not far off, a car engine sound; racing, loud.

Another engine started up; Stocker's. Stocker was leaning out of the door of the car, holding it open.

*"Hurry!"* he called. *"Hurry!"*

Mannering reached the car and almost fell in. Stocker waited until the nearest man turned the corner, and then threw a paper bag of pepper into his face. The man gasped, and flung up his hands. Stocker started off, engine roaring. As he passed the end of the road, Mannering saw more people running in the bright headlights of a car, two of them policemen.

Stocker growled: "We'll need the luck."

He drove daringly, took a corner on two wheels, swung round another almost before he had straightened up, then took a third. He drove without lights. Sitting back and gasping for breath, Mannering didn't know whether he could hear the pursuing car's engine or not. Soon he would be able to help; just now he needed a breathing space, had to have it.

They reached Marylebone Road.

"Now I can really step on it," Stocker said, and put his foot down. They roared along the wide deserted road. "I'll get you to the station, and you can find a cab. I'll be all right."

"Cheap at the price," Mannering gasped. "Thanks, Pip. Thanks – more than I can say."

"This is what you pay me for," Stocker said. "What have you got in that case?"

"Boodle."

"Share and share alike," Stocker said, and grinned. "I didn't think you'd find the girl. Any luck?"

"Not yet."

Stocker fell silent. He slackened speed when they were near Baker Street. He slowed up near the station, stopped, and leaned across Mannering to open the door.

Mannering got out.

The door slammed.

Mannering walked along, breathing normally now, until he found an empty taxi. He didn't go straight to Chelsea, but to the garage near Victoria. He removed most of his make-up there, and changed into a different coat without padded shoulders. Then he opened the suit-case with the money and jewels in it, and opened each jewel case again.

All the gems had recently been stolen; he recognised each. But the Wannaker jewels weren't here.

He locked them back in the case together with the cash, then went out, locked the garage door, and walked boldly towards Victoria Station.

Dawn was bringing the first traces of light to the eastern sky. Buses were on the move, people were stirring, London was beginning a new day.

.     .     .

No one watched the Green Street house.

Lorna was dozing, but she hadn't gone to bed. Ethel slept out, so there was no need to worry about her.

Mannering finished removing the make-up, talking all the time. His eyes were blood-shot, obvious that his head ached. Tablets and hot tea helped a little. Lorna rubbed embrocation in his knee, and that eased the pain a little. And she bathed his hand where the woman had bitten him.

"Oh, Helen Chadwick was there," Mannering said, "they moved her just before I arrived. I don't know whether Robbie had been held there as well. I've a lot of stuff that will be useful when we have a chance to go through it. Could point to Dizzy and would certainly make Wannaker thoughtful." Mannering stifled a yawn. "I'm more sure than I ever was that Dizzy's in this, you should have seen the workshop and the equipment in that cellar!"

"Stop talking," Lorna said, "you sound as if you're drunk. Go to bed."

"Yes, dear. And when that trap-door opened—"

"Go to *bed*."

"Yes, dear," repeated Mannering. "I wonder what did rouse the copper? Hope I didn't hurt him too much. I wonder . . ."

He felt as if he would never be able to sleep.

He kept muttering and thinking of all that had happened—and all the time he could see Helen Chadwick's eyes, as they had looked at him when she had challenged them to *help* her. What kind of help was he being? He had given her the impression that he couldn't fail.

He wouldn't be able to make another effort like tonight's; he'd made his chance but it hadn't succeeded. It might lead to another move, but he couldn't see one. His head, his knee, even his nerves wouldn't allow much more action. Would they?

Blue eyes, beautiful, compelling blue eyes seemed to be speaking to him, pleading, beseeching. *"Help me."* He had promised her help, he had to find her.

Lorna was saying something.

Lorna was making him take a pill; a sip of water. Was he a child? Beautiful blue eyes, beseeching, frightened eyes, and Helen had reason for fear. A girl had been killed in mistake for her. What other motive could there have been for May Sharp's murder?

He dropped off to sleep.

.    .    .

The policeman who had grappled with Mannering in the garden of 103 Courtney Street had a tender patch around the region of the solar plexus, but that was all. He was still excited, an hour after the thief had escaped, for it was his first personal encounter with a bad man in fifteen years. He had already repeated his story to the sergeant and to a Divisional Inspector; and when Superintendent William Bristow of Scotland Yard arrived, for a further account, he almost stammered in his eagerness to get everything exactly right.

"... and when I saw that residents of the neighbourhood were giving chase, sir, I gave another long blast on my whistle and entered the house, having in mind the possibility that other men accomplices of the first might still be on the premises. But what I found, sir, was . . ."

He finished his story.

"Now show me round, will you?" Bristow said.

They passed the bedroom door, where the woman was now sitting in an easy chair, with a policeman and a police officer sitting with her, tea and sandwiches on a tray, an electric fire burning.

She talked of a man in a blue mask, and seemed too frightened to lie.

The blue mask might be Mannering's; he'd been known to use one. It looked like a Baron job; and when Bristow saw the workshop downstairs, he knew that the burglar had really broken up a gang; a favourite Baron gambit.

Bristow left the woman and went into the study. Here, flashlights dazzled them, men searched for prints, others were measuring . . .

"That's *exactly* as I found them, sir," the constable said, and his voice was almost shrill with excitement. "Lying just like that, bound hand and food, and with their throats *cut*."

In fact, each throat had been slashed savagely, each man must have died instantaneously.

.      .      .

"It was awful," the policeman gulped. "I've never seen anything like it in my life before, sir."

"I can believe it," Bristow said grimly.

He looked down at Ben. He knew both Ben and Lanky Dan, but not by those names. After another talk with the woman, he was quite sure that these were the men for whom Mannering had been looking.

If Mannering had been there, this could get him hanged.

"Right," said Bristow, "now let's check a bit."

He talked with the Divisional men, but was thinking of Mannering. He had a sick kind of feeling, because the indications that this was a Baron job became clearer with every discovery he made. But he wouldn't act too quickly, he'd made the mistake of moving too quickly against the Baron before. But this, he knew, could see Mannering hanged.

.    .    .

Lorna heard the telephone ring. She left the canvas, because she couldn't settle this morning, anyhow. John was still asleep. She knew that he had been more worried than usual the night before, and from the time she had woken she had been half fearful of a telephone call from Bristow. As it hadn't come by now, it probably wouldn't. One of Stocker's men had brought the Austin here; it was outside now.

She heard Ethel saying: "... Well, he's still in bed, sir, Madam said — "

"I must speak to him." That was Stocker's voice. Lorna recognised both the voice itself and the harsh note in it — not really like Stocker's.

"Hallo, Pip," she said, "is it really urgent?"

"Desperate," Stocker said. "I'm coming round, have him awake by the time I arrive, will you? He might have to leave London in a hurry."

Stocker rang off, abruptly.

All the fears which had been latent in Lorna's mind came rushing to the surface.

.    .    .

When Stocker arrived, Mannering was up, in a dressing-gown, drinking tea, feeling better than he might have expected. It was eleven o'clock, he'd had

135

five hours' sleep. He felt reasonably fit: his hand hurt a little, where the woman had bitten him, and Lorna had put a plaster on it. Lorna was on edge, and he didn't blame her. Stocker didn't raise false alarms.

Ethel brought him to the study door; and closed it. Stocker, in grey, looked everything that his message had suggested; hard-faced, hard-eyed, so worried that worry was almost fear; and usually he covered his feelings well.

"There's no point in beating about the bush," he said. "It's the worst shock I've had in my life. I still can't believe — "

"No beating, no bushes, remember," Mannering murmured.

Stocker flashed: "It's a hell of a thing to be funny about! How you — " he broke off. "Oh, to hell with it. I always thought this was a devil of a case, as filthy as they come. Now I know. Since when did you appoint yourself Lord High Executioner?"

Mannering didn't speak.

Lorna put a hand on his arm, tightly.

"I know they killed May Sharp, I know you meant to avenge May, but not *that* way," Stocker growled. "I still can't understand why — "

Mannering broke in, his voice as calm as if they had been talking about the weather.

"Mistake somewhere, Pip. If you mean the men and the woman and Courtney Street, they were hale and hearty when I left them. I was going back to get one of them, I wanted a little chat." He managed to sound normal all the time. "Facts."

Stocker said slowly: "Listen, John, I can be fooled, but not this time. You were in the house, no one else was. The police found the woman alive, the two men with their throats cut. My men have been snooping. The bodies were found soon after we'd left. That's the truth of it. Don't ask me to believe — "

He stopped.

"Pip," said Mannering gently, "I'm not asking you to believe anything, I'm telling you the simple facts. I didn't kill them. They were alive when I left." He groped for and found his cigarettes, lit one automatically. The full significance of this news hadn't yet struck home, but he was beginning to feel numb.

Lorna held her breath, as if breathing hurt.

"Someone else must have been in the house," she said, heavily.

"That's right," agreed Mannering.

"Listen, John," said Stocker roughly. "I know you have to tell me that. I won't say I don't believe you." He seemed to find words difficult to get out. "But see it my way. I'm a private-eye. I get my living that way. I was waiting for you outside that house. I can make a case out for doing that, and satisfy the police. I don't *know* that you burgled the place, I was just waiting for you. But it's my living, and I've a conscience, too. Sooner or later the police are coming to talk to me about this job, they know my angle, and they're going to ask me what I know. I can lie. But supposing I lie, and they find that out? I'll stick with a murder charge. I could be judged an accessory. For my own sake I ought to talk and for my conscience's sake I ought to talk. But I can stall. I can be somewhere where the police can't find me until you've had time to get away. If you didn't cut their throats, it will give you time to think and decide what to do."

He stopped.

Mannering felt Lorna's grip on his arm get very tight. Then she turned away as if she couldn't bear to look into his face.

Had she looked, she would have seen the curve of his lips, the glint in his eyes, which seemed to reveal the real heart of him.

"That's right, Pip, it would," he agreed. "But it's

not going to. I didn't kill them. *I wasn't there last night*. Tell Bristow what you like, but you can't tell him you saw me, that you recognised me. Can you?"

Stocker said heavily: "Oh, you were disguised, but I met you there by appointment, I knew you would be there. You can't get out of it that way." He was impatient.

"Pip," Lorna said, abruptly, "if he goes into hiding, it will be like a confession of guilt."

"As if he didn't know," Mannering growled. "And I thought he was a man worth knowing! The first squeak of danger, and his blood turns to cold water." Bleak laughter was still in his eyes. "All right, Pip, do what you think best. Tell Bristow that you were there. Confess to being an accessory. See where it will take you. In jail for a while, that's almost certain. And it would force you to shut your business down, make you a marked man for life." He paused. "I wasn't there. If necessary I can prove an alibi. Can you?"

Stocker didn't speak.

"I wasn't there – you weren't there," Mannering murmured. "That's how it is, Pip."

Stocker hesitated. Lorna seemed to be pleading with him to agree. It was impossible to guess what he thought. He moved towards the window, fresh-faced, frowning, the burden heavy on his shoulders. He stood very erect, and when he turned round, his eyes were almost accusing.

"All right," he said. "I'll lie – for a while. But not for long. I want proof that you didn't cut their throats."

"What you really mean is that you want proof of who did," Mannering said.

He fingered the sticking plaster which covered the mark of a woman's teeth.

# 18

## CALL FOR HELP

MANNERING closed the door on Stocker, and turned
to face Lorna. His smile wasn't as buoyant as it had
been; he would not have smiled at all but for the need
to try to ease Lorna's desperate fears.

"Not good," he said.

"Good," echoed Lorna, with hopelessness in her
voice. "It's all so — "

"Odd!"

"Don't try to make light of it," Lorna said sharply.
'It's too ugly, too — deadly. How long do you think
Pip will hold out?"

"For as long as Bristow holds off the real pressure,"
Mannering said, "and that will depend on whether Bill
thinks I was at the house last night."

"He's bound to."

"Don't let's assume that the trap-door's opening
yet," Mannering said dryly, "and that the rope — "

*"Don't!"*

He could understand her anguish; he could understand anyone who felt frightened, now. He was
frightened, too. He had tried to talk lightly of the
trap-door of the gallows, and it had reminded him of
the fall through the darkness and into the pit; and the
fear which had clutched at him then. Now, it clutched
Lorna.

Who had killed those men?

Had anyone besides the woman been at the house
while he had been there? He knew that the answer
could only be yes — yet he hadn't had a clue. Every
sound he had heard had been explained, but some of
the explanations had been false. He had been watched,
and at the crucial moment the killer had struck.

"What are you going to do?" Lorna asked, and forced herself to speak quietly. "Can you do anything?"

"I've those papers, remember," Mannering said, "and some lists to study." Except for the documents, everything he had brought from Ben's house was at the garage in Victoria, but now he had to do more than hide it from curious eyes; he had to make sure that Bristow couldn't find it if he searched the flat. Evidence that he had been to Courtney Street had become evidence of murder. "Get them out," he said, "I'll take them away."

"All right. But John —"

"We'll get through," Mannering said with a confidence he hoped would make her spirit lighter. "We've had it as bad before, and —"

"It's never been like this."

She was so emphatic, so certain, that he didn't answer. It was worse than it had ever been because Stocker could give evidence. Before, all the evidence found against the Baron had been circumstantial. Now he had to persuade, convince, or blarney Stocker into silence.

"You get the papers, I'll get dressed and take them away," Mannering squeezed her arm.

"All right," Lorna said again.

As she went into the study, she glanced out of the window. Mannering saw her flinch, and didn't need to ask why. He didn't speak of it, even half an hour later when he had the brief-case in his hand, and was ready to go out. But he knew that she had seen a man watching the house.

He went downstairs.

There was a detective officer from the Yard, who made no attempt to conceal his presence.

Mannering walked towards his lock-up garage, unlocked it, took out the Rolls-Bentley, and drove off lowly. Another Yard man, in a Wolseley, followed him.

Now he knew that Bristow had found reason to suspect: and every moment might herald disaster because there was no telling how Stocker would behave under pressure.

It wasn't easy to act normally; to drive to Hart Row as if nothing had happened. He greeted the silvery-haired Sylvester who was in charge while the shop's manager, Larraby, was away on sick-leave. It wasn't easy to sit at the desk, wondering how to get rid of the evidence once he had studied it, without the police finding out.

They might pounce at any moment.

For the first time he was able to study all the facts and figures on the papers stolen from Wannaker, all with Wannaker's New York address on them. These gave details of the amalgamation of British and American companies. No doubt at all, foreknowledge would do a lot of harm to the principals – and make a fortune for whoever was in the know.

But the *Financial Times* showed no movement in the shares; no action had been taken, yet.

It would be like the unknown Dizzy to wait until he could make a dazzling coup.

Dizzy –

The name had come, months ago, from a man Mannering had tried to frighten into talking.

"He'll make you dizzy . . ." the man had sneered.

It had reached Bristow in much the same way. It had become a name which was a household word in the East End of London, too. If a little crook was held by the police and he wanted to be funny, he would sneer:

"Look out, Dizzy'll be after you."

So Dizzy had grown into a legend, without a real personality or other name, without an identity except

that built up in the minds of the police and of Mannering. There was no certainty who worked for him, only
certainty that there was a man, that he was known as
Dizzy, that he kept his fingers on the throbbing life of
London's crime – and of crime in Paris, Rome, Madrid,
New York. If legend were to be believed, he was a
world-wide racketeer, extorting protection money from
little men and big men in the crime business.

And only once, in the clash with Mannering, had he
or his men come off second-best. But none of them had
known him, none had been able to say for certain that
they worked for Dizzy, only that they thought they did.
It had been proved, then, that many of the crooks were
frightened because of Dizzy. And if Dizzy would kill
ruthlessly, as Ben and Dan had been killed . . .

That was the alarming, the terrifying thing; they had
been lying there, helpless, unable to move more than a
finger; and he, Mannering, had left them like that. Then
someone had gone in, softly and silently, and used the
knife. They must have seen him enter. At some point
just before their death they must have seen this man –
this man or woman, it could have been a woman – coming with the knife. They must have expected help.
Then, at an awful moment, their hope must have turned
to horror; they must have writhed and twisted and tried
to avoid the awful slash.

He had arranged for May Sharp to stand-in for
Helen, and May had been murdered in the same way.

He had made those two men helpless, and they had
been murdered.

These things were heavy on his mind, as well as the
fear that at any moment Bristow might come to question
him; or to say that Stocker had changed his mind.
Stocker was shaken, and who could blame him? The
man to blame was sitting here, going through these
papers, searching almost desperately but with a grow-
ing hopelessness. But for the insurance angle he would

ever have used Stocker; he would have worked on his
own, as always in the past. But Stocker could have
been, *had* been, very useful. He was sound and reli-
ble — but frightened in case he were charged as an
accessory. If he made a statement to the police, he
would stand a chance of getting away without serious
trouble.

Mannering finished studying the papers, put them in
a large envelope, and addressed it to Wannaker, c/o
Poste Restante, G.P.O., The Strand. He posted it, but
all he might need to remember was imprinted indelibly
in his mind.

The telephone rang.

He started; stared; and waited. His man would
answer it first, he would get warning if this were from
Bristow.

There was a tap at the door.

"Hallo?"

"Mr Jeffrey Wannaker would like a word with you,"
said Sylvester.

"Put him through," Mannering said.

"Very good, sir . . ."

"Mannering!" Jeff almost shouted down the line.
'Say, John, listen, *she's safe*."

Mannering said slowly, unbelievingly: "Who's safe?"

"Don't be crazy, you know who I mean! But I can't
tell the world, she's still under suspicion, isn't she? I
want some help, John, I want to know where to hide
her until those guys at Scotland Yard know that she
had nothing to do with May Sharp's murder."

        •          •

So Helen Chadwick was free, and the Baron had done
nothing towards it.

        •          •

"Where is she now?" Mannering asked, very quietly

"In a hotel in Ealing," Wannaker blurted ou
"Been there since last night. But she can't stay f
long. *Do* you know any place where she can hide?"

"Not off hand," Mannering said. The world seeme
full of people who wanted someone to hide from th
police. "What's the address?"

"The Pimperne Hotel, Waverley Street," Wannak
told him. "John, this is real urgent, she — "

"Is she all right?"

"She's tired and she's scared but I guess she's a
right," Jeff said. "You going to hurry?"

"I'm going to hurry," Mannering promised. "Wa
there, Jeff."

He rang off, and sat quite still.

There was a line connecting all the things that we
happening; the Wannaker family, the Chadwick
Dizzy, the murders; everything. What was the lin
What made everything fit into the same puzzle? It woul
be easy to think that they were parts of two differer
puzzles, but he wasn't convinced.

Why murder May Sharp?

Why kill the two men at Courtney Street?

Why involve him in hiding Helen from the polic
Was that a silly question? In a jam, wasn't Jeff goin
to approach him as the obvious man to help?

He thought of Helen Chadwick again. Bristow ha
said that she might have fooled him, Mannering, tha
she might be connected with the crimes. Well, why no
She had telephoned for him, and waited for him — an
she had been with the dead woman. He didn't know
no one could know, at what time May had been killed

His heart beat faster.

Supposing Helen had been framed — as he had been
for last night's killings. Remember that someone ha
waited until he'd gone, then killed — and it could hav
been someone who knew who he was.

Who had cause to hate him? Who would hate with such bitterness that he would plan to have him hanged? Whom did he know possessed of a ruthlessness that would enable him to work that way?

Who but *Dizzy*?

The name, the legend, the bogey-man whom he had bested once.

If Dizzy were planning to trap him, to slip a rope over his head and draw it tightly round his neck, that might explain the murders last night. It *might* explain why Jeff Wannaker was asking him to go to the Pimperne Hotel, Ealing, to —

Jeff made out that he had fallen in love with Helen at first sight; but had he? Or were they old friends? Was that just an excuse to made his attitude plausible? Were they working together, to confuse and bewilder him.

Dizzy was international.

Jeff Wannaker travelled the world on his father's business.

Mannering lit a cigarette. He heard a bell ring in the shop; someone was coming in. He grew tense, until he heard Sylvester talking quietly, and knew that it was a customer. He drew hard on the cigarette. He knew that he was at the crossroads; that a wrong turning here might be a wrong turning for good.

He began to smile.

That smile would have done Lorna good.

He picked up the telephone, switched it through so that he had a line to the exchange, and with great deliberation dialled Whitehall 1212. He heard the ringing sound, and then a break and the clear voice of the girl operator.

"This is Scotland Yard, can I help you?"

"Superintendent Bristow, please."

"Yes, sir, who is speaking?"

"John Mannering."

145

"One moment, Mr Mannering, I'll put you through."

Mannering waited, and drew a photograph of Lorna closer to him. It was a superb likeness; and she hadn't changed in five years. He gave her the grin.

"Who was it said that the best means of defence is attack, sweetheart?"

Then Bristow said: "Hallo, John, you there?"


19

## CAUTIOUS BRISTOW

"HALLO, Bill!" greeted Mannering, and sounded as bright as if all things in life were lovely and he hadn't a care in the world. "How are you this morning? Caught any bad men?"

Bristow was obviously taken off his guard.

"Chirpy, aren't you?"

"Well, why not?" asked Mannering, and chuckled; and actually felt like chuckling. "I'm in the middle of a fight and liking it."

"Mind you don't get hurt," Bristow said. Obviously he didn't know what to make of the call, and was being very cautious.

"I'm going to get hurt," Mannering said. "But what matters is who's going to get hurt most. Ever heard of Dizzy, Bill?"

"I'm busy," Bristow said abruptly, "if you haven't anything serious to say — "

"Plenty! Come and see me, will you? Or rather — " Mannering paused, and knew that he had caught Bristow's interest again. "Let's meet somewhere on the way to Ealing. What about a drink at the Globe, Hammersmith."

Bristow said slowly: "I don't get this."

"I don't want everyone to know how friendly we are," Mannering said, "I'd rather they thought that you were highly suspicious of me." He chuckled. "Bill, I think I'm being framed. The Globe, in half an hour — we'll have time for a couple."

"Your story had better be good," Bristow said. "All right."

"Shall I tell your chap outside not to worry about following me?" asked Mannering brightly, "or had I better give him a lift?"

"You let him do his job," Bristow growled.

Mannering left the shop five minutes later. The Rolls-Bentley was in a bombed site car park nearby, and Bristow's man was standing by the side of his car, close to it.

He was a beefy, massive six-feet-one.

"Hallo, Gilbert," Mannering said brightly, "you're going to have a tiring day. I'm going out to the Globe, at Hammersmith, to see Mr Bristow."

Gilbert was stolid. "Are you, sir?"

"Yes. You'd better tag along."

"I see, sir."

Mannering beamed, and went to the Rolls-Bentley, climbed in and drove smartly towards New Bond Street, which was thronged. He was held up as he turned into it; turned left then left again into Oxford Street. Mood was the oddest thing he knew; and there was nothing wrong with his mood now. He liked it. He knew that it was a false exuberance which would soon fade, but while it was with him he could enjoy it. It came because he believed that he had seen the one threat connecting all that had happened — a campaign against him, by Dizzy.

Who *was* Dizzy?

Approaching Marble Arch, Mannering saw the traffic speeding up; and the Yard man went behind a bus.

Mannering put on a burst of speed, beat the red lights, and then shot the car along the Bayswater Road. Gilbert was nowhere in sight. Mannering chuckled, and lit a cigarette with one hand, which was foolish while at the wheel, and ten minutes later pulled up near the Globe, at Hammersmith, an old-fashioned pub built of blackening brown brick and with a lot of elaborate iron work round it and a granite globe on top; a Victorian delight. It was also a comfortable pub where the food was good and generous, the hospitality genuine, and the beer had a true hop flavour. He didn't see Bristow's car. He waited outside until Gilbert came up, trying to drive and look about him at the same time. Mannering waved. Gilbert appeared to jump two inches, and his car swerved before he regained control. Soon, they were standing side by side.

"Feeling all right?" asked Mannering, kindly.

To his credit, Gilbert was grinning.

"They've always *told* me about you," he said. "Now I know what they mean."

Mannering chuckled.

Bristow came up. They went in, ordered whiskies and soda, and took them to a corner by a window they couldn't see through. No one took any notice of them.

"Now, make it snappy," Bristow ordered.

"And may all your snaps be good ones," Mannering said earnestly, and drank, and grinned. "Bill, my last words were the *raison d'être,* so to speak. I'm pretty sure I'm being framed, and I should think Dizzy's behind it. First — "

"Listen," said Bristow, "have you seen the newspapers? The early evening editions."

Mannering looked blank. "No. Why?"

"I don't quite know," Bristow said, "I don't know how much of you I can believe in. I never have." He took a folded newspaper from his pocket, and unfolded it slowly, deliberately. He watched Mannering

148

all the time, and Mannering stared at the racing news on the back, the guide to form; and then watched Bristow turn the paper over, keeping the headlines upside down to Mannering. Bristow handed it across the table.

He was looking for reaction.

Mannering looked down. The headline screamed:

## DOUBLE MURDER IN ST JOHN'S WOOD
### POLICEMAN ATTACKED

Mannering glanced at it, and then looked into Bristow's eyes. He seemed more puzzled than bland.

"Well?"

Bristow said slowly: "John, listen. I don't think you would kill them. I can believe that you're being framed. But why did you go there?"

"*I* haven't been there," Mannering said, and managed to speak as if the very idea were fresh and bewildering.

But Stocker may have talked already.

Bristow stubbed out a cigarette and lit another before he spoke again. He stared at Mannering, and when the cigarette was alight, went on gruffly:

"Tell me the truth, and I may be able to help. Keep that denial up, and I'll have to come for you. Once the hunt is on, it'll be out of my hands. Tell me the whole truth, John. Why you went, what you found, what happened?"

He was almost as persuasive as Mannering.

He probably thought there might be an outside chance of getting a statement.

Mannering began to smile, faintly, crinkling his eyes at the corners, turning up the corners of his lips.

"Oh, no, Bill! You get worse, that isn't even subtle. I wasn't at the place. What makes you think I was?"

Bristow said: "The two men were Ben and Lanky Dan. I've identified them."

This was the moment of greatest danger; the moment

when the wrong expression in Mannering's eyes would tell Bristow that he already knew. Mannering had been waiting for it, was ready for it. Surprise, incredulence and then dismay showed one after another, and he liked to think that each was beautifully convincing.

"You almost convince me that you didn't know," Bristow growled.

"All right, keep the joke up," Mannering said abruptly. "I wasn't there, I didn't know about it. It's a pity it came just now, I thought you might be in a mood to co-operate. But if you've some crazy idea that I've been round using a knife we may as well break it up."

"I came out here to see you, I don't want a wasted journey," Bristow said. "Give. You say you think you're being framed. Don't you think that these two men were killed so as to have a chance to pin a murder on to you."

"I don't."

"All right," Bristow said again. "Give."

Mannering said: "I had an excited telephone call from Jeff Wannaker half an hour ago. He's got Helen Chadwick. He says he thinks she's under suspicion for the May Sharp murder, and wants me to find a place to hide her. They're at a hotel in Ealing."

Bristow said: "Where's the frame?"

"If Jeff Wannaker wants to have me convicted of aiding and abetting Helen to hide from the police, this would be a way."

"And what else?"

"Helen called me to the hotel when May Sharp was dead. Remember what happened? I *said* that there were two other men, but could I prove it? Did they leave any traces? Any prints?" Bristow didn't answer, but Mannering knew they hadn't. "They knew Helen would send for me, and they let me walk into the trap. Then I told them I had the Wannaker jewels, but no one's asked me about those jewels since. Ben and Lanky Dan and the others seemed to have forgotten that I exist. They've found the jewels somewhere else, or they always had them and were after Helen Chadwick for a different reason. Dope on the big financial deal, perhaps."

Bristow said: "Could be. Go on."

"Helen was the bait to get me to the scene of May Sharp's murder. Is she being used as a bait again?" asked Mannering softly. "I want to go and find out. I *don't* want to be followed by your happy working men. Let me go alone. If everything's clear and above board, I'll get the girl away. She may be willing to tell me something she wouldn't tell you. I'll tell you where we're going and where I leave her. But I don't want a man on my heels in case I'm being shadowed by a Dizzy man." Mannering stood up and finished his drink. "Play it your way, Bill, but this would get results, I think."

"Where is this place," demanded Bristow.

"The Pimperne Hotel, Waverley Street, Ealing," Mannering added. "I looked it up, it's just off Ealing Common."

Soon he was outside, striding towards the Rolls-Bentley. Gilbert was already getting into his car, and Bristow was at Mannering's side.

"Must I say it again? If Jeff Wannaker's there with Helen they may tell me what happened, and I'm more likely to get the story than you are. A break, Bill, just one break, that's all you have to give me." He stopped by the side of his car.

"Who's giving the orders?" Bristow growled.

Mannering's eyes gleamed.

"Do what you damned well please." He jumped into his car. "We ought to know soon whether Jeff Wannaker and Helen are in this up to the neck, or whether they're being taken for a ride."

He started the engine, let in the clutch, and moved

off. Bristow didn't speak. Gilbert pulled up just behind Mannering, and Bristow got into the Yard car, which moved with Mannering into the stream of traffic heading for Goldhawk Road, and then Ealing.

Mannering didn't know what Bristow would do.

He almost forgot Bristow; it was as if he were blinded by a pair of magnificent blue eyes.

Bristow and Gilbert didn't follow.

## 20

## YOUNG LOVE

THE Pimperne Hotel was so close to Ealing Common that from its windows one could see the spreading trees, the children playing, the dogs frisking and the old folk sitting and talking or strolling along. Mannering noticed all this as he stopped the Rolls-Bentley at a corner, then hurried towards the hotel, which had a large sign up.

PIMPERNE PRIVATE HOTEL
HOT AND COLD IN
ALL ROOMS.

RESIDENTIAL.

It looked like a large house which had been converted. The white front door stood open. He ran up the four stone steps, glancing over his shoulder as he went. No one was there.

A little man with iron-grey hair and a pleasant expression appeared from a door marked *Private*.

"Good afternoon, sir."

"Good afternoon. Is Mr Wannaker here?"

"The American gentleman," said the grey-haired man, smiling. "Yes, sir, he's in Room 5, that's on the first floor. Allow me to show you the way. He said he was expecting you and asked me to bring you right up."

"I can find my way," Mannering said, and smiled back.

"Oh, it's no trouble, I assure you."

Mannering fought back the desire to run ahead, and wished he could understand his own strength of feeling. Fear for Helen? Or for himself? She might still be in danger; and this might be another trap for him. He had been called to the other hotel, and to a corpse; Ben and Dan had been killed to make it look as if he committed the murders; but no one in the house had known that he was Mannering.

Had they?

That was the moment when a possibility he hadn't considered before flooded into his mind. He had no time to ponder over it or to judge its significance, for the grey-haired man reached a door which had a brass '5' on it, and tapped sharply.

Jeff Wannaker answered: "Who's that?"

"Mannering," called Mannering.

"Oh, that's fine," cried Jeff, "that's wonderful!" The door opened and he stood there beaming.

Helen Chadwick was just behind him.

.        .        .

Helen showed no signs of hurt or injury. She looked tired, and perhaps because of that, her eyes had an unnatural radiance. Mannering had never seen such eyes. He felt more relaxed, almost sick with the sense of anti-climax. There had been no need for fear.

"Hallo, Helen," he said, "things work out well

sometimes, then." He shook hands, and she forced a smile. The tiredness seemed genuine, not really a sense of strain. "Have you seen your brother?"

"No." She closed her eyes. It was as if a shadow had passed beneath the sun. "No, but they said – they said he was all right."

"Who did?"

"Listen, John," Jeff Wannaker broke in, "Helen's so tired she can hardly keep her eyes open. We want to get her somewhere safe, where she won't have to worry. Maybe this is the best place, maybe you can think of somewhere better. Questions can come afterwards. Any ideas?"

Mannering hesitated.

"Yes," he said. "Come on. We can talk in the car."

.        .        .

Lorna had a small cottage not far from Kingston, close to town but buried in the country. They used it occasionally for week-ends, and the two old family servants lived there. Mannering knew that they were away and the cottage was empty.

It was less than an hour's drive from Ealing.

A car followed, and only Gilbert was in it; Bristow appeared to be giving him the break he asked for.

Helen kept dozing.

Jeff kept talking.

"This is the way it happened, John. The night she was taken away from that hotel in the West End she was drugged – just a shot in the arm. She went to sleep and didn't know a thing that was happening. She woke up in a room she hadn't seen before, and was locked in. That so, honey?"

"Yes," Helen answered.

She was sitting in the back, with Wannaker. His arm was round her shoulders, and she was nestling her head on his. She looked tired out; Mannering could just see her when he leaned forward to look at the driving mirror. She hardly seemed to know what she was doing.

"Then a woman came and talked to her, and afterwards the guy named Ben did the same." Jeff caught his breath, and Mannering thought he patted Helen's arm. "Now don't you worry, honey, Ben won't come after you again, don't you worry. I'm going to stay right here with you until I know what's happened and the police have caught those guys."

She said: "I want to find – Robbie."

"We'll find him, honey," Jeff said, with hearty confidence. "Don't worry. Say, John, won't we find him?"

"We aren't giving ourselves any rest while looking for him," Mannering said.

"See that, Helen – we're on the way!" Jeff switched quickly from that angle. "This woman and Ben wanted to know where the jewels were, where Robbie had put them. But Helen was good – that's what you'd expect, John! – she made them realise that she just didn't know."

Mannering said:

"Is that all they wanted to know, Helen?"

"Why, yes."

"Sure?"

"I'm positive," Helen said.

"What else would they be after?" Jeff demanded.

That was the first time that it seemed possible to Mannering that Jeff didn't know anything about his father's financial plans.

"Forget it," Mannering said.

There wasn't much traffic. Mannering was touching seventy, and intangible things were keeping pace. Fear. The danger that Stocker would talk, and name him. The danger that it would be proved that he had burgled

the house, that it could be proved that he had killed
Ben and Lanky Dan. The penalty for killing crooks
was the same as the penalty for killing anyone; death
by hanging, a trap door beneath one's feet, a jerk, a
fall into darkness — as he had fallen once.

The threat from the Yard had never been closer;
greater.

And Jeff Wannaker was talking like a callow boy
fresh from school, who'd never been in love before.
That oozed out of his voice, showed in his manner.
Mannering was almost sure that it glowed in his eyes.

"And what happened after Helen had convinced
Ben and the woman?" Mannering asked, and tried to
keep the sarcasm out of his voice.

"Why, they released her," Jeff cried, marvelling.
"They took her away from that house, wherever it
was, and gave her another shot in the arm. When she
woke up this morning, she was in that hotel. She'd
been taken there by car, and put to bed. What do you
think of *that*?"

It sounded phony beyond words. In fact it sounded
so fantastic that there was a nagging whisper in Mannering's mind — that it might be true. Could anyone
think up a story like this and tell it? Wouldn't they feel
sure that no one would believe it?

"That's just what happened, honey, isn't it?" Jeff
asked eagerly.

"Sure, that's the way it happened," Helen affirmed.
"I can't understand it, I just can't understand. They
were brutes at first. The man Ben" — she caught her
breath. "He really scared me. But it was only talk.
They said they would use a whip on me, and went out
for a while. When they came back they were —
different."

Phony? Fantastic? True?

"*Ben* was different?" asked Mannering.

"Yes," Helen said, and her voice was low-pitched,

156

as if she found the effort of speaking almost too much for her. "Yes, it was as if he'd been convinced that I didn't know, that he agreed it was a waste of time asking me any more questions."

Mannering saw the turning he had to take for the cottage. He slowed down, and gave the Yard man plenty of warning that he was going to turn left. After turning, he drove more slowly. He snatched a glance at Helen. She was leaning back with her eyes half closed, head on Jeff's shoulder. As Mannering turned his head, Jeff moved his right hand away from her, quickly.

"And that's all?"

"That's everything," declared Jeff. "This morning, she telephoned you but a maid told her you weren't in, and so she called me. I came right here, and when I knew she was okay, I called you. Listen, John, how long will it be before the police give up this crazy idea that Helen may have known something about May Sharp's murder?"

"How do you know they think so?"

"The Press told me," Jeff declared. "It's true, too. How long will they keep it up?"

"Not long," Mannering said, and added: "You might consider going to the police and telling them the whole truth."

After a pause, Jeff said: "Sure, that's an idea. Sure. You think your friend Bristow" — he appeared to ponder deeply. "Say, John, Helen and I are prepared to trust your judgment on a thing like this, aren't we, Helen? You talk to Bristow, and if you think it would be a good thing to tell him where Helen is, okay, you tell him."

Mannering slowed down. They turned off this road along a by-road with hawthorn hedges on either side, and then came within sight of the cottage. This was creeper-clad, with a rustic fence, a small lawn and a mass of colourful annuals which were vivid in the sun. There was no drive up to the front door.

"This the place? Why, it looks swell," Jeff enthused. "Isn't that so, honey?"

"Jeff," Helen said. "And Mr Mannering." She was sitting very erect. "Don't forget the thing that matters – finding Robbie. I *can't* believe that he stole those jewels."

Yet something in her tone suggested that against her will she was beginning to believe that he had.

Mannering helped her out of the car, took them to the cottage with its tiny rooms and beamed ceilings, gables and its lichen. He had a key on his ring, opened the door and showed them round. He was there for half an hour, and when he came out, Gilbert was standing behind some bushes; a Yard car was further away from the cottage than Mannering's, just out of sight.

"Having a day in the country?" Mannering asked brightly.

"That's right, sir," Gilbert said, "I'm staying here until I'm relieved. I've a message from Mr Bristow for you, sir."

"Ah. What message?"

"I'll quote him, sir. 'Don't play any tricks, and go straight back to the Yard'," Gilbert paused and moistened his lips; he looked very strong, very naïve; a countryman if ever there was one. "And also, if you know where Pip Stocker is, will you telephone the Yard right away?"

. . . .

There was nothing really surprising about Bristow's interest in Stocker. It was even possible that Stocker had talked, and this message was Bristow's way of warning Mannering.

Mannering drove back to London with too much on

his mind, and no nearer understanding – but nursing an idea he didn't like.

Helen's story seemed more phony the more he thought about it, but she was well, unhurt, just tired. She might tell a different story under cross-examination, but he doubted it. If it were true, why had she been released? She had stayed at Ben's house, the woman there had given her a meal, and then she had been drugged and taken away – and left at the hotel.

Why?

Who had used pressure on Ben, to arrange that? Ben's boss? Dizzy?

Why should he? They had gone to a lot of trouble to put fear into Helen, and made a good job of it. Why had they been prepared to believe that she didn't know where the jewels were?

One answer stood out: they'd already found them, so Helen couldn't be any more use; consequently there was no point in holding her, except that she could have given evidence against them for assault and kidnapping.

He had to get it straight.

First, she had been taken away from Ben's house. Then, Ben and Lanky Dan had been murdered. They were the only two Helen had seen besides the woman. It was almost as if she had been released by someone who had already known that Ben and Lanky Dan would die.

Slowly, Mannering warned himself. . . .

Someone had known that they were going to die; but how could anyone have known that the house was going to be raided? He had seen it as an unpremeditated murder; the killer had seized a chance to kill them both and have a stranger blamed.

*Who?*

Jeff Wannaker? Jeff could have lied and be luring him to another trap, but he seemed moonstruck with young love. Jeff could still be fooling him, couldn't he? The one part of the story, of the incident, which it was so hard to believe was Jeff's fondness of Helen; they'd made great progress; he could hold her, hug her, caress her, and she took it calmly, almost for granted.

Were they really comparative strangers?

The more Mannering thought of Jeff, the more he thought of all the Wannakers. Elaine's emotional tantrums, Saul Wannaker's attitude towards his son, and his fear that Elaine would be killed if he continued to brief Mannering.

Look at the situation as it really was.

Mannering was suspect, and the danger would get closer. He needed to find Robbie Chadwick and the jewels; he had to find Dizzy and the murderer of Ben and Lanky Dan. The first three mattered only because they might lead, they should lead, to the fourth. He had to find a murderer or the rope might go round his own neck.

The behaviour of the Wannakers, all the Wannakers, was odd. That put it mildly. He needed time to think about them, find out more about them, visit them. He needed to stop Elaine from acting, to find out just how much Saul knew. How far did the financial business come into it? Was that distinct from the jewel theft, or part of the same haul?

He bought two evening newspapers when he reached Hammersmith Broadway; headlines about the murders screamed at him. He glanced at the stop press, and felt as if he had been struck.

### ST JOHN'S WOOD MURDERS
Scotland Yard anxious to interview Percival 'Pip' Stocker, private inquiry agent, who is believed to have been near the scene of the murder last night. Stocker, aged thirty-seven, is reported to be out of London.

# 21

# BRISTOW GROWLS

MANNERING looked across the desk at Bristow.

Shadows appeared on the Yard man's desk as the
branches of the plane trees by the open window stirred
under the freshening breeze. The office was quiet, but
there were the noises of the Embankment and of the
River outside.

Mannering had told Helen's story.

Bristow was looking at him, cigarette in the corner
of his mouth, as if trying to see into his mind. There
was no telling what he might do. He might decide he
had sufficient evidence to hold Mannering —

Bristow seemed to relax.

"So you're going to tell me that you believe that
yarn." He almost sneered.

"All I've said is that it's so absurd I can almost
believe it," Mannering answered mildly.

"I wouldn't believe it unless I'd seen it with my own
eyes," Bristow said. He stood up, and drew nearer.
"Listen, John. You found out Helen was at that
house in Courtney Street. I *know* you were told so.
That's the house where Ben and Lanky Dan were
murdered."

Mannering felt his heart thudding.

"Pip Stocker's wife told me," Bristow said, and
stopped.

Mannering had to sit still; to face him; to meet his
eye without giving anything away.

"Pip Stocker's wife heard him telephoning you and
telling you, last night. Pip told her he thought you
were going to visit the house. Pip went out. He was
driving his green M.G. A green M.G. was used to take
the burglar away from that house. Remember?"

"I wasn't there to remember," Mannering said flatly.

"You were there. You ran from the house, attacked a policeman, ran to a car. Stocker drove you away. Now Stocker's in hiding because he doesn't want to be made to give evidence against you. He daren't lie, and he knows it. He can't stay away for long, either, but he's giving you time to get in the clear. His wife's off her head with anxiety." Bristow stopped, and moved back a little. His movements, his words, the expression in his eyes were all deliberate; menacing. He had guessed the truth, and the only question was whether he had evidence.

If he hadn't he would get it when Stocker was questioned; and Stocker would not stay away long now that he knew that the police were after him.

Bristow lit another cigarette. His eyes looked glittery, saying a lot of things that he wouldn't utter.

"John, give Stocker a break, give yourself a break. I know you were at the house. *I* know that you wouldn't kill that pair — not that way. If they'd died in the explosion it would have been different, but you wouldn't kill cold-bloodedly. But you were there and you can tell me exactly what happened. With a start like that, I can get after the killers. Without it" — he paused, lit another cigarette, and let smoke dribble through his nostrils. "Without it, we'll have to hold you. See? And people without my sentimental idiocy won't think you wouldn't have killed them. They'll say you were there, and used that knife."

"Bill," said Mannering, "you're all cock-eyed. And you've no evidence to hold me."

Bristow suddenly flashed into action, smacked a clenched palm into his other hand, shook his fists and roared:

"To hell with you! You knew where the girl was,

you broke in and rescued her. Young Wannaker was with you and he took the girl to the hotel, while you stayed behind to see if the Wannaker jewels were there. That's the story, that's the truth, and Stocker will know, he was outside waiting for you. He helped your get-away.''

''It's a waste of energy, Bill,'' Mannering said, ''and a waste of good ideas. Go and try it on Jeff and Helen. He'll wish you to perdition because Helen's asleep by now, but you won't mind that. Wake her up, shoot the questions at them both, find out if they'll change their story or if they saw me. Go and ask them, Bill.''

Bristow glared, then backed away, picked up his cigarette, and stubbed it out.

''When we pick Stocker up,'' he said, ''we'll have all the evidence we want. If you told the truth now you'd have a chance. If you wait — '' he paused. A different expression came into his eyes. He groped for another cigarette. He looked startled, almost alarmed. ''Listen,'' he said in a strangled voice, ''Stocker had better be all right, we'd better not find his body in the river with his throat cut.''

. . .

Mannering left the Rolls-Bentley outside the Green Street house and walked towards the front door. A different Yard man was watching him from the doorway of an empty house. Another was at the corner; and a third had followed him from the Yard.

He walked slowly upstairs.

The door opened as he reached the landing, and Lorna appeared. She looked pale and harassed, dark hair fell over her forehead. She didn't speak, but looked at Mannering tensely. He slid an arm round her waist as they went in.

163

"An army's outside," he said.

"I know: And Quinn's is watched back and front too."

"It would be."

"I've been out," Lorna told him. "Just shopping. I was followed. And — I'm sure that the telephone's tapped. Men have been working on the cable in the street."

"It'll be tapped at Quinn's, too." Mannering smoothed down his hair, tried to make himself look less anxious; but the anxiety went deep, and there was no way to ease her tension. "An all-round pressure, which hurts. Where's Ethel?"

"I sent her off, I couldn't stand her chatter."

"Let's make a cup of tea," Mannering said.

"John." They were in the kitchen, and Lorna picked up the kettle. "Have you heard from Stocker?"

"No."

"Seen the evening paper?"

He nodded.

"Once Bristow questions him, it will be all up," Lorna prophesied.

Mannering watched her turning on the tap, and lit the gas so that it was ready when she had finished. The gas popped and hissed. She put the kettle down heavily.

"My sweet," Mannering said, deliberately. "It looks as if Stocker's missing."

She jumped.

"No!"

"Bristow guesses what evidence he could give," Mannering said. "Bristow's in a mood when he could really believe anything — even that I'd kill that pair and Stocker too, to save myself from jail. If Stocker turns up, I'm sunk, and if he doesn't turn up and they find his body — "

He stopped.

Lorna went to the window. She stood very still, very upright. He watched the stillness of her face.

"Is there any way round it?" She spoke without looking at him; as if she couldn't bear to meet his eyes.

"A possible way. The Wannakers and Helen Chadwick. Helen's been released."

That startled Lorna again, and she turned round.

"The story sounds phony." Mannering passed it on in brief outline. "It could be true, but Jeff and Helen seem much more intimate than I'd expect. I'm going to tackle the Wannaker family tonight. I want to know why Saul dropped out, whether he's paid off someone who could have queered this deal of his, whether he and Jeff would kill so as to make sure they could pull the deal off. And is Robbie Chadwick missing because he discovered something about the Wannakers?"

The telephone bell rang. The way Mannering moved told Lorna how raw his nerves were. He went into the hall ahead of her, and she stood in the doorway. He picked up the receiver.

"Mannering here."

"Hallo, Mannering," said a man with a voice which he didn't recognise. "I thought you'd like to know that the police have just taken Stocker's body out of the river. His throat's cut."

He stopped.

He chuckled — and rang off.

Lorna came hurrying across the hall, as if fearful of disaster.

"What is it? John, what is it?"

He told her.

.   .   .

He waited until it was nearly dark, then went into the bedroom and made up again. This time, Lorna

165

wasn't with him, she was packing clothes and essentials in case he had to stay in hiding for some time. As he worked, he became more like the man who had raided the house in St John's Wood; but he was thinner, and he didn't pad his body.

It took him half an hour of tense work.

He wound the tool-kit round his waist, and then went into the bedroom. The case was ready, a rucksack which he was able to fasten on to his shoulders without feeling the weight too much.

"How do I look?" His grin was almost rakish.

"If you can get away from here — "

"Darling, I'm going to get away." He kissed her suddenly, fiercely, then set her aside.

He went to the window of the study —

The light was out.

He opened the window without making a sound, and peered down into the open space at the back. One of Bristow's men would be down there, watching; but it was dark and no light came from the nearby houses. Mannering climbed out of the window, groped up, got a hold on the guttering and hauled himself up.

He reached the roof.

He heard Lorna's whispered: "God keep you," and heard the faint sound as she closed the window, then moved cautiously, spread-eagled on the roof, until he reached the chimney stack. There, he stood up, cautiously. He was making for the roof of a house some distance away, one which wouldn't be watched. But it was a quiet night, and nearby sounds would be heard down below, he mustn't make any noise.

He reached the next house.

A new sound came through the quiet — a car engine, close by. He looked down. A car turned into Green Street, its headlights flashed on and shone on the watching Scotland Yard men. Then they went off, and the car slowed down.

Holding on to a chimney stack, Mannering looked tensely into the street.

Two men got out of the car, and one of the watching men approached them. They met on the pavement. Mannering was nearly sure that one was Bristow. He heard the faint murmur of voices floating up; as the voices of men conspiring. He wanted to stop and make sure that it was the Yard man, but instead he turned slowly towards the next roof.

In five minutes, he was on top of the last house. There was a sheer drop from the edge to the concrete a hundred feet below. He unwound a thin rope, made a loop at one end and fastened this round a chimney stack. He fastened the other end round his waist, then lowered himself over the edge and started to move downwards. He pressed his feet against the wall, to keep steady.

He stared towards the cloudy sky, and blessed the clouds.

Then he looked down.

If Bristow suspected that he would cut and run for it, to make a final bid to prove his innocence, this end of the terrace of houses might be watched. Mannering couldn't be sure that he wasn't going to drop into the arms of waiting police.

22

## ESCAPE TO WHAT?

MANNERING was about ten feet from the ground when he stopped moving. Just here a batten was built against the wall, to strengthen it, and he found some support. He twisted round so as to look downwards.

The darkness had been a boon but had become a danger. Men might be waiting there.

He heard nothing.

Then he saw someone moving back from the corner. The man was there for a split second before he vanished – just a shape and a pale blur of a face.

Mannering stopped moving, then took three tiny phials, loaded with ammonia gas, from a pocket.

No one else appeared.

For a moment, Mannering dared to wonder if he had been dreaming; then he heard a faint sound from that corner of the house; so two men were there. Bristow had anticipated his move, and was countering it.

Mannering lowered himself, very slowly.

He reached the ground.

They hadn't pounced, yet; they were probably waiting until he reached the corner; and there would be men at every corner.

The thudding of his heart and the racing of his pulse, both quietened. Here was a crisis, and in any crisis he was habitually cool, almost cold; and detached. He went towards the street corner, moving briskly, as if it didn't occur to him that anyone was there.

He turned the corner.

Men showed up against the street lights, a powerful torch was shone into his face, dazzling him; and Gilbert said in a harsh voice:

"All right, Mr Mannering, give it up."

Mannering tossed a phial into his face, heard the gasp as it struck, the little sound of the fragile glass breaking, followed by the coughing. Another man leapt at him, only to catch a phial in the face and stop, reeling. But there were other men behind Mannering, rushing now, and he swung round. They were only a few yards behind him, and one shouted:

"Whistle, Fred! Blow – "

Mannering tossed another phial, which hit the first

man, and leapt at the second. Luck still fought for him. He bowled the man over, and spun round and raced towards the far end of Green Street and the Embankment. He reached it before anyone had even started after him; it had been a swift, complete triumph. Exhilarating! He passed a man and a girl who stared after him, but they didn't matter, no one mattered except getting away until he could mix with a crowd. He swung right, on to the Embankment with its lights glistening on the shifting surface of the Thames, then up the next street; and, soon, into a main road where there was a flow of traffic, buses, taxis, people in their hundreds.

He hailed a taxi.

A policeman watched him.

"Waterloo, in a hurry," he said to the cabby, and climbed in and slammed the door.

.    .    .

From Waterloo, he travelled by bus to Victoria Station, and then went to the lock-up garage. He had never known a time when he hadn't a car handy, for emergency; but he hadn't put the Austin back.

He locked himself in, and went through the wads of money and the jewels which he had taken from Ben's house. He had missed nothing on his previous search. The money was just money, the jewels were real but they were not the Wannaker gems.

They would be safe here if they were safe anywhere; so would his ruck-sack. He left it all, and went out. No one could have followed, no one except Lorna and Larraby, his manager, knew about this garage. But as he stepped out, his heart was thudding with all the old, familiar fears. Fears of what might happen were always worse than anything else.

He reached Victoria Station.

He could get a cab and go straight to the Wannakers' apartment, but couldn't try to break in yet. He had to find out if the apartments were being watched by the police.

At least he could begin to think again.

He telephoned the block of flats and played helpless. He wanted a Mr Watson, but wasn't sure what flat number he was at − 17 or 27 − there was a seven in it. 27, he knew, was below the Wannakers.

"We haven't a Mr Watson, sir. There's Mrs Watkins, Flat 19, but with a seven − well, no, there's no name like that. Mr Pilsener, Flat 27, Mr Hayward, 17 . . ."

Mannering said he was awfully sorry he had worried her, and rang off. He called again promptly and in a different voice asked for Mr Pilsener.

The Pilseners were out.

Mannering took a cab to Mayfair square, and walked from there to Park Lane. He didn't limp, because someone might have reported the 'limp' last night.

Who knew that Stocker was able to give evidence against him? Who knew, if anyone, that a dead Stocker would heighten the suspicion of the police, and would start the hunt for the Baron in earnest?

From the beginning, Jeff had been on this job; Saul Wannaker too; Elaine − and Helen Chadwick. It was easy to forget Helen and her hunt for brother Robbie. It was as easy to forget about her Robbie, because he had never been seen. It was almost as if he had never existed, but Mannering had seen his photograph, knew that he was very like Helen except for his eyes. The obvious thing, the probable thing, was that after being fired by Wannaker for making a pass at Elaine, he had tried to get his own back by robbing Wannaker, but − the obvious often misled.

He needed a suspect; a man − or a woman, remember, or a woman − who could be Dizzy. That was, who ould have influence on criminals in several countries, who was a master fence, and a man who gave crooks protection' through his organisation.

It wasn't exactly a young man's job or a young woman's. Helen was how old? Twenty-five or so. Was that old enough? Jeff? Jeff, at twenty-seven, was mature in some ways if so adolescent in others. Elaine? Saul Wannaker?

Supposing Saul Wannaker and his Dresden-china wife were involved, *and Jeff knew*. Supposing Robbie Chadwick had robbed Dizzy, and then been made to suffer for it, not realising the enormity of the crime he was committing. It would explain Robbie's disappearance, could also explain why Saul Wannaker had backed out. And if Jeff suspected his father of being a crook, it would explain Jeff's manner, too.

Would he have thought this up if he hadn't been at his wits' end to find Dizzy? To save himself?

He turned into the street where the Wannakers' apartment building was.

Among the three men nearby was Gilbert, standing near a street lamp. Gilbert looked at Mannering with that casual yet thorough look of a trained detective, and then turned away; he did not even suspect that the passing man was disguised.

Mannering turned the next corner.

Getting into the block would be almost as dangerous as getting out of his flat had been.

.  .  .

The police were at each corner. Knowing he had doubts about Saul Wannaker, Bristow would warn his men that a man — he wouldn't name Mannering — might try to break in. He would warn the watchers to expect any means of approach; to look for a cat-burglar, or for someone sidling in by a side door — for any stranger. If the block were being watched like this, then the actual apartment would be, too; no one would get in without being noticed.

Mannering went back to Park Lane, and entered Hyde Park under the watchful eye of two policemen. A few people were walking along near Rotten Row, some were lying on the grass. There was a constant gurgle of talk, laughter, giggles. The night was warm, in the disguise Mannering felt too hot; uncomfortable. He walked more slowly. A girl, on her own, watched him coming, and he could see her smile invitingly.

He had to get inside that block of flats.

On his own, he would be suspect; with a companion it would be different. He began to smile—

.       .       .

She was quite young, not unattractive. It was just a pick-up, and she was nervous. Arm-in-arm, they walked along the street towards the building. Gilbert saw them. They turned into the building. A commissionaire was in the doorway, he approached slowly, watching, puzzled.

"Good evening, sir."

"Goot eeffening," Mannering said, in a voice which was heavy with accent but quite clear. "Mr Pilsener, he lives here, yes?"

"Oh, yes, sir, Apartment 27."

"T'ank you." It was so easy; too easy? The girl, well-briefed, and doing well, clung to him.

"I'll take you up, sir."

"T'ank you."

A Yard man was sitting in the luxurious entrance hall, he watched, without much interest. The commissionaire took Mannering and the girl up.

The lift bell rang as they stepped out.

"I find my own way, t'ank you," Mannering said.

He gave a quick smile, and led the girl along the passage.

"Thank you *very* much, sir," the commissionaire said.

The lift took him down.

"Come on," said Mannering, and hustled the girl to Number 27. She stared when he took the knife out of his pocket and began to force the door.

"I don't understand, what—"

"You don't have to understand," Mannering said. "You just wait in here, I'll come for you soon." The door opened, and the girl gaped. "In you go," he said, and hustled her inside. He looked round, swiftly; no one was here. "Make yourself at home, and wait for me. Understand?"

"Yes, but—"

"In here, honey," Mannering said.

He opened the door of the living room, and she went in. He gave her a cigarette, and she drew nervously on it, as if regretting her folly; she was a pretty little thing.

"Now take it easy," Mannering said, taking out his wallet. "You won't get hurt, and here's a fiver. You'll get another if you wait until I come. If you don't—"

He didn't finish.

He could knock her out; or bind and gag her; and have her hostile when the time came to leave. Or he could trust her not to give him away. If she left before he came back, the last thing she would do would be to tell anyone how she had got here; she would get off as soon as she could.

"It's easy money," he said, and kissed her lightly, and went off.

In the passage, heavy velvet curtains were drawn at the windows.

He pulled them aside and opened the window. There was a small balcony, and another immediately above it. It couldn't be better—but he had to be quick. He

173

climbed up, clung to the bottom of the top balcony, and hauled himself over.

If one of the watching police glanced up at that moment he would be finished.

There was no sound.

He forced the catch of the window, opened it, drew the curtains aside, and stepped in. He knew where the Wannakers' apartment was, and did not need to pass the landing, the lift or the stairs to reach it.

He neared the door.

A bell rang, and the drone of the lift sounded faintly. The lift doors were just out of sight. Mannering waited until he heard the doors open and shut, then turned his back, as if going towards another apartment. He heard footsteps, but soon a door opened and closed, and silence fell.

Mannering reached the door of the Wannakers' apartment with the pick-lock in his hand. A detective was just round the corner—

Mannering used the pick-lock with the swift ease which came so naturally to-night. Metal scraping on metal seemed so loud that no one could miss it; but no one came. He opened the door, and stepped into the square hall. The doors leading off it were all closed.

He pushed this door to, and stood and waited. The detective at the landing might have fooled him, he had to make sure. The watching men might have seen him too, and be on their way up.

Nothing happened.

He heard the muted sound of voices in the room immediately opposite the front door. Wannaker and Elaine? He moved towards it, but before he touched the handle, there was a different sound. He spun round on his heel.

The door of the kitchen opened and the black maid came out.

# 23

## ELAINE'S STORY

THE girl was three yards away from Mannering. She came straight out, humming; then stopped, horrified. Her mouth opened very slowly, until it couldn't open any wider. He could see the pink of her tongue. Her eyes seemed to grow larger and larger. Her big bust rose as she drew in a terrified breath. Any moment she would shriek, and wouldn't be able to stop herself.

Terror showed in her eyes, she tried to turn away, but she was stiff as with dread.

Mannering clapped a hand over her mouth, stifling the cry, held her tightly for a moment, and then put his lips close to her ear.

"Don't worry," he whispered, "I won't hurt you."

She began to tremble.

"I won't hurt you at all, don't worry." He kept his hand over her mouth, and drew her towards the kitchen. It was very warm. A radio played on a muted note, and there was a ball of red knitting wool on a table near an American magazine open at a romantic story.

"Just do what I tell you, and you won't be hurt at all," he said. "Keep quiet. Absolutely quiet." He took his hand away cautiously, ready to clap it back if she looked like screaming. She didn't, but kept her mouth open. He was reminded of the way Ben's wife had bit him.

Every moment was horror for the girl; the one part in this that he hated. It was kinder to be quick. He struck her sharply on the nape of her neck, and held her as she slumped down. He tied her hand and foot to a chair, then gagged her. Then he stepped towards the door, listening; but there was no sound.

He went into the bedroom.

He didn't know where Wannaker kept the 'safe' suit-case but it was more likely to be in the bedroom than anywhere else. The rest of the luggage was here – fine quality, pale brown leather, looking spick-and-span. The huge wardrobe was crammed with expensive dresses, a smaller one with American suits. Like everything about the Wannakers, this spelt money.

He couldn't find the suit-case.

He pulled up a chair, stood on it and found it on top of the wardrobe, which had a recess there. He lifted it down, put it on the bed, went to the door to listen, but heard nothing except that faintly muted radio. He went back to the case, and opened it. Wannaker had shown him the trick, it wasn't difficult; he managed with the knife.

Some money, and a few papers were there.

So were Wannaker's jewels.

.    .    .

There wasn't any doubt. Mannering had sold these to the American only a few weeks ago. He knew each stone – beautiful things that were scintillating and giving off a dozen different colours, little streaks of fiery light. Even then, he felt the hypnotic pull of their loveliness; they seemed to be alive.

He didn't stand and hold them for long, but put them back, slowly.

He closed the suitcase and lifted that back to the wardrobe.

He looked round, and saw Elaine Wannaker's hand-bag on the dressing table. He opened it, and looked closely at all the oddments, make-up, purse, money, keys. Then he found a piece of screwed up paper. He smoothed it out, and read a scribbled note, just brief scrawl which set his heart pounding. It said: 03 *Courtney Street.*

So Elaine Wannaker had known about Ben's house. Had she ever been there?

Had she been there the previous night?

The front door bell rang.

.     .     .

The Wannakers would expect the maid to open it. They would wait expectantly, and when the caller rang again they would go to find out why Mary hadn't opened the door. They'd discover her sitting in the kitchen, bound hand and foot.

Mannering moved slowly towards the door.

Another opened, there were footsteps; and then the front door opened.

"Good evening, Mr Wannaker," a man said.

"Why, it's Superintendent *Bristow*," Elaine Wannaker exclaimed, from close behind her husband.

.     .     .

Men entered the hall, then another room. The door closed. Mannering crept out and reached the drawing-room in time to hear Wannaker speak.

"I don't want you to misunderstand me, Superintendent," Wannaker said dryly, "but I'm no longer in need of your help."

"You may need it more than you realise," Bristow said tartly. "I didn't come to talk to you about that. Have you heard from Mannering?"

"Why, no."

"You probably will," Bristow said. "I want to warn you, sir, that there is a call out for John Mannering, and that if he gets in touch with you, your duty is to telephone Scotland Yard. Do you understand?" He

was torn between giving Wannaker the respect tha
High Authority said that he should have, and letting
the American know that he hadn't much time for him

"I understand that only too well," Wannaker said
"Hell's bells, you're after *John*. What's he been doing
to get himself in trouble?"

"I'm not at liberty to disclose that, sir." Bristow
was very formal. "But it is extremely important tha
you should inform Scotland Yard if he gets in touch
with you. I've come in person to make sure that the
message is delivered *and* understood."

Wannaker said dryly: "That's very kind of you
Superintendent, I appreciate it."

Whatever Bristow had come for, Mannering knew
it wasn't that. Bristow was cunning as a fox. Had he
actually come to search? Would his next suggestion be
that he ought to look round?

"I don't want any more mistakes in this case,"
Bristow said, still formally. There was a pause; an
awkward kind of pause. Then: "When did you last see
Percival Stocker, Mrs Wannaker?"

.     .     .

Mannering stood close to the door, ready to move at
any sign that they were coming out; to lock the door
and take his chance of escaping through the window
But as that question came, all thought of escape disappeared. The question seemed to burn itself into his
mind.

*"When did you last see Percival Stocker, Mrs Wan-
naker?"*

.     .     .

There was a sound, as if the woman had gasped at
the words. Silence followed. Then Wannaker coughed,
an unmistakable sound.

"Superintendent Bristow, I don't like the tone in which you speak to my wife. Honey, you don't have to answer that question."

"Mr Wannaker—"

"You heard me." Wannaker's voice was sharp.

Bristow said, grimly: "I've heard a lot of things from you and your son in the last few days, Mr Wannaker, and I don't like many of them. Your wife is known to have been associated with Percival Stocker during the past few days. She is known to have seen Stocker yesterday." He paused, but no one interrupted; it was as if both of them sensed the significance of what was coming.

Bristow said: "And Stocker was found, murdered, this afternoon. What business did you have with him, Mrs Wannaker, and when did you last see him?"

Silence. . . .

Then Wannaker said in a gentle voice: "There's the door, Superintendent."

Bristow hadn't a warrant, or he would have said so then. Mannering moved, swiftly, and was back in the bedroom. Then Bristow and his men left; but they wouldn't go far.

.    .    .

The Wannakers were still in the drawing-room. Mannering was at the door again; it was ajar and he could hear the slightest sound.

"You'd better tell me all you can, honey," Saul Wannaker said. "I can help your memory too. You've been making a deal with Stocker. One of his men telephoned me. I went to see him. He was ready to sell his boss short, and I paid him for proof."

So it was coming out.

Elaine's breath came heavily. Mannering could imagine her standing there with her great eyes wide open, her pink face looking like fragile china.

"Oh, Saul," she said in a strangled voice, "Saul, I did what I thought was right, honestly I did. Stocker told me he knew where to find the jewels, he said he'd found them. And he—he scared me. He sent a man to attack me because I wouldn't agree at first. That man with the knife." She paused, and Mannering thought grimly that Percy Morino had attacked her; so Percy worked for Stocker. So had Ben and Lanky Dan and—

"I just *had* to obey," Elaine cried. "So I went to see him, Saul. I saw him last night at his house. He said that he would hand me back the jewels *and* release poor Helen Chadwick if I—"

She broke off.

"Go on, honey, tell me just what happened," Wannaker said in that same voice. But Elaine didn't go on at once. She gave Mannering time to digest this news and all that it implied. Stocker had had the jewels, Stocker had released Helen, Stocker had been able to make a deal with Elaine, who had been at the murder house.

Then Elaine said, huskily:

"I had to tell him about your big oil deals, everything you're planning. He said he could make a big pile on the market if he knew. Saul, I just had to tell him, he would have killed that poor girl, and he would have—"

"Sure, honey, you had to tell him," Wannaker said suavely, "but give me the real reason, won't you? The real reason why you just *had* to tell Stocker about all that."

Was there a sneer in his voice: a lash of contempt? Of hatred?

Elaine didn't answer.

"Why didn't you tell the Superintendent?" asked Wannaker, "why didn't you explain that you're in love with another guy, and you just *had* to save his life?

180

also. That's true, Elaine, isn't it? You bartered my trade secrets for Robbie Chadwick's life. You stole my papers. Did you take the jewels, too?"

"No!" she cried. "No, I didn't!"

"Let's have the truth now, honey, we've had the lies too often."

There was a long tense pause.

"Saul," Elaine said in a choky voice, "I just had to save Robbie's life. But that was everything. I wasn't going to keep deceiving you, from the time he stole the jewels I knew he was no good. But I couldn't let him die."

"Do you know where he is?" asked Wannaker, in a voice with no expression.

"Yes, I know, but—"

"And weren't you going to him to-night?"

"I was going to help him get out of England, just with some money, that's all. I wasn't going to go off with him, but I had to help him. If the police catch him they'll know that he stole the jewels, I couldn't let that happen to him." Her voice had changed, she sounded weary, emptied of emotion. "You don't have to believe me, Saul, but after this I would have finished with him."

"After this, you'll finish with him all right," Wannaker said in the same deadly voice. "And I'll beat the hide off him. Where is he?"

"Saul, don't make it any worse, don't—"

"*Where is he?*"

"He's at an out-of-town hotel, at a suburb called Ealing," Elaine said, "the place where Helen and Jeff were. But, Saul, don't go there, you'll hate yourself if you go there."

"Then I'll hate myself," Saul Wannaker said, and now he sounded vicious; savage. "I've got plenty of hate. What's he call himself?"

"Robbie—Robbie Clark."

"I'll go and see Mr Clark," Wannaker growled.

There were footsteps, then a variety of sounds; what might have been sobbing; next a thudding noise, as if someone were rolling about. Mannering opened the door cautiously — but caution wasn't needed. Saul Wannaker was reeling under the blows of his fragile-looking wife. Elaine was beating at his face, kicking, hissing at him. Wannaker was covering up and backing away, hadn't the strength of will to strike back and stop the assault. Mannering had. Mannering struck her as he had the maid, and Elaine collapsed like a punctured balloon. With blood welling up from a scratch in his cheek, and gasping for breath, Wannaker made an ineffectual move towards the door.

"You come later," Mannering said.

He left Elaine locked in the wardrobe and Wannaker in a closet, and hurried downstairs.

The girl was still in Pilsener's apartment. They went downstairs together, hurrying until they reached the hall. From there until they were out of sight of the watching police, they moved slowly arm-in-arm.

At the corner of Park Lane, Mannering hailed a taxi. As it slowed down, he put ten pound notes in the girl's hands, kissed his hand to her, and climbed into the cab.

"Victoria," he said clearly, and sat back. As soon as the girl was out of earshot, he changed the instructions. "Make that Ealing Common, will you?"

A talk with Robbie Chadwick and, later, Helen might clear up everything. But Stocker —

Who had killed Stocker?

# 24

# ROBBIE CHADWICK

EALING was silent beneath the blanket of the night. No lights burned in Waverley Road. Mannering walked from his taxi towards the Pimperne Hotel, feeling a strange exhilaration, an almost suffocating excitement. He slipped inside the gateway of the hotel, then peered up and down; he heard nothing, saw nothing.

He went round to the back. A dim yellow light burned at one window, that was all. He examined the catches of the ground floor windows, none of which was shuttered. There was no need to climb, these would be easy to force. He opened a blade of his knife and slid it between the two window frames, touched the catch, and pressed. After a moment's resistance, the catch clicked back and the window gave a hollow booming sound.

He waited; but nothing stirred.

He prised the bottom window up with a screw-driver, until he could get his fingers under it, then thrust it up. It gave a groaning kind of squeak, but it was soon over. He paused again, head raised, eyes glinting.

No sound came.

He climbed into the room beyond; his torch showed lounge chairs and couches. He found the door, the hall where he had been before, and the little office; the shutter was down at the hatch, the door was locked.

He opened it with his skeleton.

There was the entry in the registration book: Robert Clark.

He was in Room 7.

Mannering went upstairs keeping close to the wall by habit, making only a faint sound on the carpet. The hotel was so quiet that it was like a house of death.

The landing walls showed up faintly, and a yellow light burned outside a door marked *Toilet*.

Room 7 was in the other direction.

Mannering turned towards it, stood outside, and listened; then he used the pick-lock. Would the bolt be shot? He turned the handle and pushed, and the door yielded. He stood with it open an inch, listening with that intentness which put even thought from his mind. He heard someone breathing.

He stepped in and closed the door very gently; it made a faint click.

Someone stirred, on the bed, and then went still.

Mannering didn't move.

He could just make out the shape of the bed and the dark ball on the pillow; a man's head. Had the man woken?

Mannering believed he had; there was a different note in the breathing, which was just as steady but more shallow. Then he heard a faint rustling sound. He told himself that Chadwick was reaching for a gun, which might be under the pillow or at the chair by the side of his bed. Anyhow, he was awake, fearful, ready to fight.

Mannering switched on the light.

It blazed, dazzling the man in bed; his eyes opened wide for a second, then closed and opened again. He rolled over and snatched at a gun lying on the chair as Mannering flung another phial of ammonia.

.        .        .

The chair banged against the wall, the gun slid to one side, but didn't fall. The man on the bed lay back, gasping, eyes running, nose red, lips parted. He had fair hair and a clean-cut look, but it wasn't Robbie Chadwick, it was Pip Stocker.

Mannering moved slowly, a man in a dream, until

184

he reached the chair and picked up the gun. He backed away. It wasn't any mistake, this was Stocker, who was supposed to be dead of a cut throat. Stocker, who had made a secret deal with Elaine Wannaker.

.  .  .

Stocker's eyes still watered and his mouth and nose looked red, but he was able to sit up, breathe freely, and talk. He looked at a man who might have been a stranger but whom he would guess was Mannering. He was regaining his self-control but nothing of his courage. He hitched himself further up on his pillows, and looked at the knife in Mannering's hand.

Mannering said:

"You'll talk fast, Stocker, or I'll slit your throat and laugh while doing it. Hurry."

"Listen, John," Stocker said, "I know who you are." His voice was hoarse, frightened. "I know you've put this across me, but take it easy. We can do a deal, there's always time for that."

"Forget it," Mannering said. He used a voice so different from his normal one that Stocker narrowed his eyes, as if touched by doubt. "I want to know everything. Then I'll decide what to do with you. I'm not Mannering, but I'd rather kill you than let you make trouble for Mannering."

Stocker said thinly: "You can't fool me that way, John. But I'll talk, we can do a deal!" He glanced at the knife, and licked his lips. "I tried to double-cross you, but I didn't know how good you were. We can work together. It's big business. It isn't just a few sparklers, it's *big*. I can put you on to a commercial deal tomorrow that will make you a fortune — fifty thousand pounds, easily, without any risk, all bright and legal too. You can't want more than *that*."

Mannering said: "Why did you kill Robbie Chad wick?"

"Listen, Mannering," Stocker said. He paused licked his lips, then went on: "Let's call it a day. killed Chadwick, okay. He was dangerous. He lost hi head over Elaine Wannaker, that's why he got fired I discovered that, and offered him a chance to get hi own back, but he wouldn't take it. He knew I was afte Wannaker's financial plans, and wouldn't say a word so I had to work on Elaine Wannaker. It wasn't s difficult."

Mannering said: "What about the jewels?"

"I didn't touch them," Stocker said testily. "Ber and Lanky Dan were after them, and thought Chad wick had them. Ben, Lanky and Morino were on my pay-roll. They'd orders to get documents about Wan naker's big money plans, but all they could think o were the jewels. They went after Helen Chadwick be cause they thought her brother had taken them, but he hadn't. Elaine put them aside, to sell so that she could give Robbie Chadwick a big parting present. This-this is all true, John!"

It sounded like the truth; but the knife in Manner ing's hand didn't waver.

"Go on," he growled in the harsh, assumed voice. "Who killed Chadwick?"

"It — it was in a fight," Stocker muttered. "I didn' mean to kill him. I'd kept him prisoner, wanted him to get all this dope, but he wouldn't play. He tried to escape, and — and there was an accident. So I dressed him up in my clothes, it would fool the police for a while. I needed time to get away. I thought I was safe here, how — how did you find out where I was?"

Mannering said: "Elaine Wannaker knew."

"The hellcat," Stocker muttered. "She must have followed me. She — "

"Why did you kill Ben and Dan?" Mannering demanded abruptly.

"I didn't!" Stocker cried. "Percy Morino did that, he hated their guts, and took a chance – it looked as if you were going to take the rap. He didn't know who you were, but he was around, waiting to cash in when you'd gone."

"Where is he now?"

"He's hiding in the East End, hoping it will blow over. Mannering, that's true. I didn't kill those boys, although they let me down. I was after big money, they hadn't the sense to take it. Why, they had the dope on Wannaker all the time! Elaine told me; she had to copy the details from a duplicate set. Ben and Lanky Dan had a fortune under their noses but didn't know it. Listen, John, you and I – "

"You and I nothing," Mannering moved the knife; and the sight of cold steel made Stocker flinch. "Remember May Sharp?"

"That wasn't me!" cried Stocker. "That was Ben. May was smart, she could have sent him down. He killed her and thought he could frame the Chadwick girl – was sure that would make her talk. For those paltry diamonds! If he'd listened to us, to Dizzy – "

"That's nice," Mannering said softly. "This Dizzy. Who is he?"

"He's just a name," Stocker muttered. "I – I'm part of it, and work with overseas agents. We each run a country, calling ourselves Dizzy. Listen, it's big money, Mannering!"

Mannering was seeing an office door:

*The Ling Inquiry Agency*
*Confidential Inquiries*
*P. Stocker.*
*Represented in: New York, Paris, Rome, Buenos Aires.*

"Let's make a deal," Stocker gasped. "Put tha'
knife away, *put it away.*"

"It isn't quite everything," Mannering said. "Why
the campaign against Helen Chadwick?"

"I've told you! Ben thought Chadwick had the
jewels, and she knew where they were. He was working
the jewel angle, I was on the other."

"Why did he let Helen Chadwick go?"

"*He* didn't," said Stocker hoarsely. "*I* did. I made
his wife let her go."

"Why?"

"Jeff Wannaker had gone mushy on her, and I
thought I might do a deal with Jeff," Stocker said. "So
I let her go, meaning to pick her up again if needs be.
The thing I can't understand is Elaine talking. And
knowing I was here. She's — she's smart, John." He
licked his lips. "Put — put that knife away!"

Mannering just grinned at him.

Stocker sweated: "Listen, let me go. You lifted those
jewels from Courtney Street, so you've made plenty
already. It'll pay you to let me go, if the police find me
I'll have to tell them the truth." He was quaking with
fear. "I'll have to point at you. Let's make a deal,
John."

Mannering still grinned.

Beneath the grin, his heart hammered and his mind
was in turmoil. Stocker might give evidence which the
police would believe and use against him. It could
smash his reputation, bring him to disgrace and ruin.

And Stocker was at his mercy.

Mannering had the knife in his hand.

"Don't!" gasped Stocker, "don't kill me, don't — "

Mannering felt like screaming. . . .

Then he knew he could never do it. He sweated, as
if he had passed through some great physical ordeal.
He lowered the knife and moved towards the bed. He
saw fear still in Stocker's eyes; perhaps Stocker thought

hat he was going to strangle him. He would knock
Stocker out, tie him up, leave him – and then telephone
the police. Stocker would give evidence against him
and he would deny it. After all, Stocker hadn't seen
*Mannering* at Courtney Street: had only seen a stranger.

Then Mannering heard a sound outside. He smashed
a blow at Stocker and put him out, jumped up and
opened the door.

Two detectives were in the passage, and he heard
others on the stairs. The men saw his gun, and
stopped short.

"Cut it out," one said sharply. "Put that away,
or – "

Mannering glared; but the odds were hopeless, now.

Bristow appeared on the landing.

Mannering said harshly: "Your man's in Room 7.
Stocker. That's all you want, isn't it?"

He moved the gun forward, growling:

"Out of the way, I don't want killing."

Then Bristow *slipped*.

He fell against the other two men, and they went
sprawling. He fell as Mannering rushed past them and
down the stairs. A policeman in uniform stood in the
hall, eyes rounded when he saw the gun. Mannering
fired at a spot a foot above his head, and made him
jump back violently.

Mannering raced into the street.

Bristow's car was at the kerb.

Men came running from the Pimperne Hotel as
Mannering started off in it.

.        .        .

Bristow picked himself up, looked about him angrily,
and hurried towards the door of Number 7. He took
one look inside, and began to smile.

.        .

Two weeks later, Mannering and Lorna were at the door of the Chelsea flat when Saul, and Elaine, Jeff and Helen Chadwick arrived. They had come straight from their last visit to the Yard. They knew, as Mannering knew, that Percy Morino had been caught, and that Ben's wife had seen him at Courtney Street, and knew that he was the killer. They knew, too, that Robbie Chadwick had died in a fight, that Stocker-hoping to make it look as if the same murderer were responsible, had used the knife after death.

Stocker was part of Dizzy; but not a killer. The other Dizzy agencies were already closed down.

There was an air of relaxation about the four as if an unbearable tension had eased after a long time. Helen had an air of repose which softened even the startling beauty of her eyes. She was over the worst grief, now.

"Well, we've told the police everything we can again, and they've told us plenty," Saul said. "I guess you know most of it, John."

"I've had sessions with Bristow," Mannering agreed. "But there's plenty I don't know."

"I can tell you some of it." That was Elaine, who was very tiny, very lovely, and unusually subdued. "John — Saul and I aren't going to quarrel about it any more. I was crazy about Robbie, but knew it wouldn't work out, and I tried to cure myself. But when I thought he needed help, I just had to help him. I really believed that Stocker would release him."

"Listen, honey," Saul said gently, "you don't have to talk about it any more."

"I want to talk about some things," Elaine insisted. "You can imagine what I felt when I heard what had really happened, John. But before that, when that man broke into the apartment" — she didn't pause, but Saul Wannaker began to smile faintly — "I didn't want Saul to go to the hotel. I'll tell you why. I was afraid that Jeff was mixed up in this, and I didn't want Saul to hurt. I wanted Robbie to get away and everything quieten down. If I could, I'd have beaten Saul sense- s to make him stay.''

''Someone else saw to it that I didn't get there,'' ul Wannaker said. ''As for Jeff—''

''I'm okay,'' Jeff said, with a broad grin. ''Just a y in love, I guess. But I can tell you a few things, . The moment Pa knew Elaine was in this, he cked right out. Yes, sir. That was the first time I er realised he really loved the dame. And I'm kind reconciled, now.'' His arm was round Helen's waist. Aren't I, honey?''

She looked very pale; but she smiled.

Other things were known, now. That Ben had sent note from Robbie, hoping to force Helen to talk. at Morino had been sent by Stocker, to terrify aine; that Ben, after 'small' money, had told Saul annaker that Elaine was dealing with Stocker.

They knew that Elaine had been a victim of her own ly too long, and come to see the danger from Stocker. fore he had forced her hand, she had followed him, scovered that he lived at the hotel, as Clark, and at he owned the hotel. The manager was on his pay- l—and was now on a charge.

The party left, an hour or so afterwards.

The Mannerings watched them turn the corner, then nt back upstairs, looked out of the window, saw no e in the street. A shadow had been lifted and there s nothing more to fear.

''Back to normal,'' Mannering said, ''you in the dio and I at Quinns! Which reminds me, you didn't ld Elaine to her promise to have her portrait inted.''

Lorna laughed.

''If I know Elaine, she'll be back. I want to show u something up there, though.'' She led the way up loft ladder and into the studio.

Mannering saw the panorama of London on canv
for the first time — the London he loved. He put h
arms round her, and stood looking at the magnificen
of the scene and the beauty of the painting.

Although he did not say a word, she knew that
would mean as much to him as it did to her.